D0499115

Also by Cathy MacPhail

Run, Zan, Run
Missing
Bad Company
Dark Waters
Fighting Back
Another Me
Underworld
Roxy's Baby
Worse Than Boys

The Nemesis Series

Into the Shadows
The Beast Within
Sinister Intent
Ride of Death

Cathy MACPHAIL

GRASS

BLOOMSBURY

LONDON BERLIN NEW YORK

Bloomsbury Publishing, London, Berlin and New York

First published in Great Britain in 2009 by Bloomsbury Publishing Plc
36 Soho Square, London, W1D 3QY

A CIP catalogue record of this book is available from the British Library

ISBN 978 0 7475 9911 1

The paper this book is printed on is certified independently in
accordance with the rules of the FSC. It is ancient-forest friendly.
The printer holds chain of custody.

FSC
Mixed Sources
Product group from well-managed
forests and other controlled sources
Cert no. SGS - COC - 2061
www.fsc.org
© 1996 Forest Stewardship Council

Typeset by Dorchester Typesetting Group Ltd
Printed in Great Britain by Clays Ltd, St Ives Plc

1 3 5 7 9 10 8 6 4 2

www.macphailbooks.com
www.bloomsbury.com

For Jessica Lee

'Want a Mint Imperial?' I handed over the bag of my favourite sweets to my mate, Sean.

He pushed it back at me, and pulled a Mars bar from his pocket. 'You know I hate them things, Leo. Gimme chocolate any day.'

We were on the train heading home after the Saturday match. Our team had lost 3–0, but in our minds we had not been defeated. We usually lost by a lot more than that. Nearly all our friends supported Rangers or Celtic. But not me and Sean. We liked to be different. We were Barnhill men, like our dads before us. We supported our local team, Barnhill. Or, 'Barnhill Nil', as some rotten people liked to call them.

We were well pleased that day as we headed home on the coastal railway line past Dumbarton Rock, watching the river sunset red and the whole town bathed in a pink glow.

'We're really lucky living in the best place in the world, with the best football team.'

Sean laughed. He agreed with me. 'When they were handing out luck, McCabe, God gave us an extra share.'

That's how me and Sean always were. We agreed about everything. We were best mates. Had been since Primary 1. We liked the same things . . . except when it came to Mint Imperials – but then you can't have everything.

We were just drawing into one of the stations when Sean pointed towards a wall surrounding one of the derelict factories. 'Hey, look at that.'

It would have been hard to miss what was written on that wall. Painted in giant whitewashed letters.

SHARKEY IS A GRASS

I hadn't a clue who Sharkey was, but I knew one thing. 'Sharkey's a dead man,' I said. 'They should have added RIP – Rest in Peace.'

'Or rest in pieces.' Sean laughed. ''Cause they'll probably cut him up and drop his body bit by bit into the Clyde.'

Me and Sean are big C.S.I. fans and they'd had a storyline just like that only a couple of weeks ago.

'I wonder who Sharkey grassed on?' I said.

'Could have been Nelis, or Armour, or McCrae.'

Everyone knew the top gang leaders in the town. The drug dealers, the hard men, the bad men. Nelis had an evil reputation for doing the most awful things, and Armour was simply called 'The Man'. As if there was no other. McCrae was vile. His name would always be linked to the Sheridan lassie. She'd come from a decent family but once she'd started running about with McCrae he'd got her on to drugs. Her life had spiralled downhill, and when she'd finally had the courage to leave him she'd been found shot dead not far from McCrae's house. No one leaves McCrae. He had even been charged with her murder but managed to get off when two of his 'friends' had supplied him with an alibi. But no one doubted his guilt. Andy Sheridan, the girl's dad, had sworn all kinds of vengeance on him for that.

McCrae and the others always got off due to lack of evidence – or lack of surviving witnesses. No one ever grassed on them because once you did you'd be a dead man, like Sharkey would be soon.

'He's probably left town already,' Sean said.

But Sharkey, whoever he was, the drug dealers, the crime bosses, everything was forgotten by the time the train stopped at our station. We were going to Sean's house. He had a new PlayStation game and we were dying to try it out.

Sean lived in McCrae territory. Crazy, I know, that they claimed areas of the town as their own, but that was the way it was. Sean and me, we were streetwise enough to know that. But we kept back from any trouble. My dad and Sean's would have gone spare if they'd caught us having dealings with anyone connected to McCrae or any of the others.

And on the way to Sean's house we did what we loved best. We explored.

The area where Sean lived had so many boarded-up houses and derelict properties and shops, and me and Sean were experts at getting inside them. It was exciting and a bit dangerous as well. You never knew what you might find. It was about the only risky thing we did and it didn't hurt anybody. We'd sneak inside, pretend we were SAS commandos searching out terrorists, or crime scene investigators looking for clues. Always the good guys, me and Sean.

There was a new boarded-up shop to explore that

night. Azam had finally had enough. He'd given up after all the hold-ups and break-ins and vandalism to his shop. He had closed up and decided to move to somewhere less dangerous. 'Baghdad, I think,' he had told Sean's dad. 'It's a lot safer there.'

'My dad says it was a blinkin' shame,' Sean said. 'Azam was trying to give the people here a good corner-shop service. They never gave him a chance.'

It sounded like something Sean's dad would say. Like my dad, Sean's was always complaining about how the town was run by those three gang bosses.

'If Azam had paid McCrae protection money, he could have stayed,' I said to Sean. And he agreed. Everyone knew it went on. McCrae would threaten the small shopkeepers with his gang of hard men, who would break up the shop or warn customers to stay away – shop somewhere else. In the end most of the shop-keepers would pay up just for the sake of peace. But after that they would be in McCrae's pocket for ever.

'The Untouchables', my dad called Nelis and Armour and McCrae. Because the law could never seem to touch them. They got off with everything. Verdicts not guilty, or not proven.

So now Azam's once brightly whitewashed shop was

covered in graffiti – on the walls, on the door. Even on the steel panels that boarded up the windows. It was easy getting inside. Me and Sean were experts at finding a way. One of those steel panels was lying askew at the back door, and first me and then Sean squeezed through. First thing that hit us was the smell. Somebody had been using this place as a toilet.

Sean started dancing about like a cat on a sizzling hob unit. 'Hope I don't put my feet on something yucky.'

I was almost tempted to squeeze back through into the street, but my crime-busting instincts took over. I pulled out the pen-torch I carried with me (well, I did say we were always exploring) and flashed it across the ground. Just as well. Another few steps and Sean *would* have stepped on something yucky. The vandals had obviously been here already. It never took long for them to get inside any derelict properties. There was broken glass all over the floor, pipes had been ripped from the walls. There was graffiti on every empty space.

'I hear something,' Sean said.

I could hear it too. A low moan from one of the dark corners. We were always hoping to find evidence of a crime or a robbery in progress, maybe stumble across the aftermath of mayhem – a dismembered body in black bin bags strewn across the floor. So far the only thing we'd ever come across was a gold watch. We took it to the police. Got a reward too. Didn't I say we were always the good guys, me and Sean?

But here in the dark, listening to that moaning coming from the shadows, it occurred to me that right at this minute I'd rather be at Sean's playing his new Zombie computer game.

Neither of us moved. The moan became a growl. I flashed my torch towards the sound.

I thought at first it was a wild animal. All hair and teeth. It leapt at us. Me and Sean yelled and this time Sean didn't miss the yucky stuff. He sank his foot right in it.

The face became clear. It was an old man, a dosser. He was yelling like a beast.

'Get oota my place! Ya wee . . .' He threw something at us. We didn't wait to find out what it was. We had never moved so fast, squeezing out of the door almost at the same time. It was only as we were running away that we started to laugh. Laugh until we couldn't stop.

'Oh, we would be brilliant crime scene investigators,' I said. 'One old weirdo and we're off faster than a speeding bullet.'

I made a whizzing sound, and it only made us laugh all the more.

My dad picked me up later at Sean's. My dad nearly always picked me up . . . or my mum did.

'I'm not having my boy walking these streets late at night,' they would both say.

I had a great mum and dad. A great family and the best mate in the world. Sean.

That night as my dad was driving me home and I was yattering on about the match – giving him a kick-by-kick description of the game – I was really happy. Life was good.

Nothing was ever going to change that.

2

Monday morning, and I came down for breakfast all ready to go to school. My dad's face was clouded over, his mouth grim. I didn't even have to ask the reason. I had spotted the scrunched-up letter that had been chucked in the corner. Another knock-back. Another job he didn't get. He'd been trying so hard to get another job ever since the electronics factory he'd worked in had closed down and he'd been made redundant. I gave my mum a quick glance. She was at the cooker doing me my scrambled eggs on toast. She shook her head. 'Don't say a word,' her look was telling me. So I didn't.

It was my wee brother, David, who finally brought a smile back to my dad's face. David is five years old, just started school. He walked into the kitchen with a pair of blue boxer shorts on his head. My dad took one look at him and burst out laughing. 'What's the idea of that?'

David climbed into his chair and said, as if it was the most normal thing in the world, 'I'm Mr Bean. Mr Bean wears his underpants on his head.'

David was always playing at something. His games usually involved me. Me and him fighting aliens. Me and him being pirates. Me and him finding lost treasure. That morning his game was exactly what was needed to change the mood.

'You're five years old,' my dad said. 'You're in school now. What would your girlfriend say if she saw you sitting here with your underpants on your head?'

'Jessica's not my girlfriend,' David said, spluttering out a mouthful of Rice Krispies.

Jessica sat beside him in class. He had been invited to her birthday party just last week. We were always winding him up about her.

I snatched the underpants off his head and threw them across the kitchen. He immediately began to bawl. 'Mum! Leo's stealing my underpants.'

In the end he had the whole family laughing again. Typical David.

I had Sean laughing about it too when I met him at the school gates. I told Sean everything, even about my dad not getting the job. Sean understood. His dad had been in the same boat as mine. Made redundant from the same factory. But his dad had managed to get a job pretty quick. It was only stacking shelves in the supermarket, but he'd said he would take anything to get back to work.

My dad would too. Though what he really wanted was to get back into the electronic business.

'I hate to see him sitting there every day, Sean. My dad likes working.' I shrugged. 'The man's daft. He could be living off my mum and benefits but instead he wants to work.'

'And of course your mum earns so much at the hospital.'

Mum was a nursing auxiliary, but she wasn't full time, though she had applied for it.

I had such a good life. If my dad could get a job everything would be perfect. I'd do anything to get my dad a job, I thought.

'Something will turn up,' Sean said. Then he changed the subject. We'd talked enough about the dark side of life. 'Want to come to my place for your tea? I've got a great new game.'

It was always better going to Sean's. First of all there

was no David to annoy us, trying to barge into the room. Even when we barricaded the door, he would find a way. Either that or he'd kick up such a fuss, my mum would insist we let him in. 'I'll be good,' he would promise. He never was. Two seconds through the door and he was diving on us, bombarding us with pillows, wanting to play.

And secondly, and more importantly, Sean's mum didn't ask too many questions when we went out. Just told us to be careful. Not get ourselves into any trouble.

The lighter nights were coming in – late February – and after our tea we ran through the estate, checking out where we could explore next.

Over the railway bridge at the edge of Sean's estate there was a long line of empty tenement properties. Clyde Terrace. The council was planning to pull them down. They were going to build new houses here, in this prime spot that had a spectacular view right over the Clyde. But so far nothing had been done to them. They had been boarded up for months, with steel panels on the windows and doors. They looked impregnable. But that was only a challenge to me and Sean.

'Let's separate,' Sean suggested. 'You start over

there.' He nodded to the other end of the terrace. 'I'll start here. Text me when you find a way in.'

I watched him go, crouching along the walls like an SAS commando on a mission. I had to smile.

'Nobody can see you here, pal,' I was thinking. Because the back of the properties only looked on to another line of derelict housing.

It was such a waste, I thought, all those empty houses, when it could have been a great place for people to live.

Or maybe not. Nelis had taken over this area with his band of moneylenders and thugs. Most people would take out a loan just to get out of here.

I waited till Sean was out of my sight before I began to move just as stealthily towards the far end of the terrace. Every so often I stopped to tug at a steel panel to see if it might come loose. But every window, every entry was sealed tight. I was almost ready to give up – to text Sean that I was having no luck – when I spotted it. The steel corner over one of the windows was bent out as if someone had prised it open. Vandals probably – like me – trying to get in. I crouched closer and gave it a tug. It scraped across the sill, but with another pull it creaked a little wider. I could fit in there, I thought. Skinny little me? No problem. But maybe not Sean. A wee bit wider in the butt, was Sean.

I pulled my phone from my pocket to text him I'd found a way and only then noticed I had no charge in my battery.

I looked back along the line of tenements but there was no sign of my mate. Maybe he had found another way in, had tried to text me and failed and had decided to go inside by himself.

So would I then. I slipped my phone back in my pocket and took out my torch. Then I squeezed inside.

The torch's beam sent a long thin light across the floor. I moved it around and realised I was in an old kitchen. No graffiti. No pipes or wires pulled out. The vandals hadn't been here yet.

And for a split second – a micro-second – I wondered, why not? These houses had been lying derelict for months. Usually it only took days for the vandals to move in.

But the thought was gone in an instant. I was the first one here, that was all. Boldly going where nobody had gone before. A pioneer explorer in a new land. I opened the door of the kitchen and stepped into the living room. Black as pitch. My torchlight caught a picture still hanging lopsided on a wall. I peered closer. A steamer coming into harbour, gulls flocking around it. It reminded me that this had been someone's house – someone's home once. I moved further into the room.

The house was thick with silence. It seemed to me I was cut off from the world outside. Totally alone. I swept the light across the bare floorboards and immediately swept it back again.

One of the floorboards was lying loose.

I was down on my knees in an instant. Maybe, I was thinking, someone had left a box of money under those floorboards, their life savings, and had forgotten to take it with them. Or maybe a cache of stolen jewellery, or . . . my imagination went into overdrive.

Or maybe a body.

I sniffed the air. Wouldn't I be able to smell a decomposing body?

But there was nothing.

This was a definite Mint Imperial moment. I sat back, pulled one from the bag in my pocket and flicked it into my mouth.

That loose floorboard had to be significant. There had been no vandals in here, so why was the floorboard loose?

My hand was almost touching it when I remembered

Sean. Should I go back outside, find him, help him and his fat butt to squeeze inside so we could discover the secret under the floorboards together? Of all the times for my phone to have no battery!

But on the other hand, maybe there would be nothing there at all.

But it was too late to go back for Sean. I couldn't wait. He'd understand.

I reached out and lifted the floorboard free.

3

I thought at first there were snakes under there. Long, thin, silver-grey snakes, lying straight and flat, sleeping under the floorboards side by side. The torchlight seemed to dance over them. I held my breath, too scared to reach out and touch them. Hey, I'd seen too many Alien movies to trust anything long and thin and sinister in a dark place.

At any moment they might come alive, fold themselves out from under the floor, rise above me with dripping jaws – and strike!

It seemed so real, I moved back.

But everything stayed still. I realised I was sucking on my Mint Imperial like mad. I waited a moment, knew I had to find out what I was looking at. I held the torch closer and saw then that there were no snakes. No alien monsters. These were something much more menacing.

Guns.

All kinds of guns. Rifles, shotguns, pistols, machine guns. Ammunition too.

A whole stash of guns.

It wasn't rocket science to figure out what I had stumbled across. And with the realisation, everything became clear. Why there had been no vandals in this building.

No one would dare.

Once we'd come over that railway bridge, we had stepped into Nelis territory.

This was Nelis's stash of guns. Had to be. And I had found them.

I almost yelled out for Sean then. This was the biggest thing we'd ever found. Tell the police about this and we would be heroes . . .

A picture flashed into my mind.

SHARKEY IS A GRASS

If Nelis ever found out it was us who had grassed on him, we would be dead men.

But something else stopped me calling for my pal. Because maybe someone other than Sean was out there. Nelis wouldn't have left this place unguarded. Someone had to be out there. One of Nelis's hard men. And he had seen everything. Had watched me sneaking inside the building. Knew I was here. Maybe he had already warned Nelis, and him and more of his thugs were heading my way. I pushed the floorboard back in place, silently, covering the guns again. The torch was shaking in my hand.

I tried to think calmly. If someone had been left guarding these guns it was obviously someone not too bright, or they would have stopped me coming anywhere near here in the first place. So maybe he hadn't seen me slipping inside. Perhaps this watchman had paid a visit to a girlfriend nearby, or he'd sneaked off for a takeaway curry. He'd be back any second.

But it was more than the fear of any guard outside that stopped me calling out for Sean. *I* had found the guns. Just me – I was the only one who knew about them. If someone caught me, I'd be in danger.

If I called Sean in here – he would know too – then he'd also be in danger.

Too much knowledge is a dangerous thing. This was a need-to-know situation. And Sean didn't need to know this.

Couldn't do that to my mate.

I edged back, still kneeling on the floor. My eyes never left that loose plank of wood. Almost as if I was scared the guns would come out by themselves. I heard it in my imagination. Rifles cocking, machine guns rat-a-tatting in the silence. And all of them aimed at me.

It was then I got to my feet, began to back my way through into the kitchen. Only at the door did I turn and then in my hurry to get out of that place, I tripped and fell face down, cracking my nose on something hard on the floor. My nose began to bleed but I was up and running in an instant. My instinct telling me to get out of there as quickly as I could.

I was breathing hard as I squeezed back through the steel panel, sure a line of Nelis's men would be out there, waiting for me.

Was this how a soldier felt escaping from a prisoner-of-war camp?

But there was no line of angry men.

There was only Sean standing further along the terrace, looking in the opposite direction, waiting for me.

He didn't see where I'd come from. He swivelled round when he heard my stumbling footsteps behind him.

Sean called out to me.

'Where did you get to? Did you get in?'

I didn't stop hurrying away from there, pulling him on as I spoke. 'Naw, couldn't find a way. Did you?'

'Naw. Sealed up tight.' He saw the blood streaming from my nose then. 'Hey, what happened?'

'I fell.' I pulled him on.

'What's the hurry?' He glanced back at the building. 'Did you see something there?'

'Naw. It was just smelly and then I fell . . .' I just wanted to get him, both of us, as far away from here as I could. 'I don't feel good. I want to go home.'

Instantly, Sean forgot about the building, good mate that he was. He called out into the night.

'Man down. Wounded officer losing blood. Paramedics over here.'

Normally I would have laughed. But now I didn't want to waste the time. And I was afraid too, that someone might hear his shout. I didn't laugh with him.

He looked at me, and just for a split second I could see suspicion cloud his face. I wasn't telling him everything, and he knew it.

I changed the subject. 'Do you think I've broke my nose?'

He grinned. 'Well, if you have it's bound to be an

21

improvement. You've got a conk like a big potato. Maybe you'll be better-looking after this.'

We decided it would be just as easy going back to my house. And this wounded soldier wanted home. The bleeding had stopped by the time we got there, and my dad ran Sean back home. His dark mood had lifted. My dad never stayed down for long. But I went to bed almost as soon as they'd driven off.

All I feared was that someone had seen me, clocked me, recognised me. Knew what I had found.

Too much knowledge is a dangerous thing.

I vowed that from now on me and Sean would stop investigating the old houses. We'd find something safer to do – like wrestling alligators.

4

The fear had left me by the time I woke up next morning. The sun was shining and a frosty mist hung over the river. Now, in the light of day, last night seemed more like an adventure.

Finding those guns in the dark, stumbling out of there expecting any second that Nelis and all his henchmen would leap out of the shadows and grab me – you know what it reminded me of? Like when you watch a film through your fingers the first time, because you're so scared the good guy is about to die horribly and then he doesn't. So the next time you watch it you can really enjoy it, knowing he's going to be safe. It was exactly like that. I watched the re-runs of my adventure over and over and it got more exciting every time.

But share it with Sean?

No way. It was still too dangerous to share with anyone.

He was waiting for me at the school gates. He looked disappointed to see me.

'I was expecting you to have your nose spread all over your face,' was the first thing he said. 'Or at least be attached to a blood-transfusion drip.' He said it as if I had let him down badly.

I popped one of my mints in my mouth. 'My mum says I acted like a drama queen. There wasn't that much blood.'

'Overacted, I'd say.'

I longed to tell him then about the guns. It was the perfect moment to share that sinister knowledge with him. Here in the playground, waiting for the bell to ring. What harm would it really do, I asked myself?

But the words wouldn't come.

Too much knowledge – that's what stopped me. He could be in danger if he knew.

I was in danger.

My eyes glazed over – I went into dream mode – the hairs on the back of my head stood on end.

I was in danger. Maybe even now someone was watching me.

And for a moment it wasn't a bright sunny morning any more. There was darkness all around me. My mood changed. I was afraid.

'Are you listening to me?' Sean was shaking me. 'Hello! Is anybody there? Can you get dementia at your age? You just switched off there, pal.'

The sun came out. No need for me to be afraid. No one had seen me last night. We'd never go back there again. I would make like it never happened. Push it to the back of my crowded mind.

There were other more important things to think about anyway. Like the final of the school football tournament, and the new Zombie game that Sean had.

'It was my granny's,' Sean told me at break time. 'She's says it's the best ever.'

Sean always got the creepiest games and the best horror DVDs from his granny.

'Your granny's weird, Sean. Do you know that?'

He only nodded. 'I know,' he said, dead chuffed. 'You can come at the weekend and play it.'

I hardly heard him. Veronika Kuschinska walked past just then. Veronika is one of the Polish girls who has recently come to our school. Long blonde hair and beautiful white teeth. (Her dad's a dentist.) Not that I notice her much.

Sean nudged me. 'Looking at Veronika again, are you?'

'Veronika who?' I said.

Sean started to laugh. 'Veronika who! You can't keep your eyes off her in class. Talk to her. Who knows? She might not be right in the head. She might like you.'

'I'm not interested in her,' I said firmly. And it was the truth. Why would I be interested in a girl, even with long blonde hair and green eyes and perfect white teeth?

Two days later there was a shooting in the town. It was on the estate where I'd found the guns. Nelis territory. A drive-by shooting, a boy badly injured. My first thought when I heard about it was: had someone used one of the guns I'd found? Would it not have happened if I'd told the police about them?

The shooting was all the talk of the town. It sent my dad into fighting mode. 'More shootings! Here in our town! This place is getting worse.' He pulled David on to his knee, as if he could protect him better if he was close. 'One of our boys could have been caught up in that. Totally innocent, walking by, caught in the cross-fire. It doesn't bear thinking about.' He looked at Mum. 'I think it's time we started thinking of moving some-where else.'

I knew he was only saying that. We couldn't get out

of this town no matter how bad it was. Dad didn't have a job, and where would we get another house? Added to that, my dad loved this town. Leave the town with the best football team in the world? I don't think so.

My mum tried to calm him down as she always did. 'Oh, come on, Dave. You're talking as if we were living in war-torn Baghdad. This is a great place to live, and most of the people in this town always obey the law. We do.'

'*You* don't,' I reminded her. 'You nick surgical gloves from the hospital all the time.'

Behind my dad's back she waved a fist at me. I grinned. Dad was always going on about that. My dad refused to do anything underhand.

'That's not really stealing,' my mum said. 'It's only a few pairs of surgical gloves. Kept under the sink . . . for medical emergencies.' She glared at me.

'It starts with the little things,' Dad said. 'That's how it always starts.'

'I'm not goin' to start shooting people because I take a couple of pairs of gloves out of the hospital.'

My dad thought it was wrong anyway. Any kind of stealing was still stealing, he said.

My mum decided it was safer talking about the

shooting. 'Anyway, we keep our boys away from any trouble, Dave. We drop them off. We pick them up. We look after them.'

And that was true. A lot of the boys my age ran wild on the estates. No one at home to care for them – either not giving a monkey's where they were, or out clubbing themselves. I was lucky. I knew there was always some-one here for me.

There always would be.

5

I didn't get to play in the final of the football tournament after all. Total rubbish of course, leaving me on the substitute bench. I could have been man of the match. And it was all down to the Bissett Boys.

I haven't mentioned the Bissett Boys yet. They come from one of the worst families in the town and between you and me the two brothers only share a brain cell between them. But they never give me a minute's peace. As soon as they catch sight of me, they're on my tail, always chasing me. They used to come right up to the house, till one night my mum came out and gave them some serious verbal abuse. Since then they stay back from the house. Instead, they wait on corners for me. Why? It's only because I don't support Celtic . . . and I don't support Rangers. That's a good enough reason for them. I always do my best to avoid them – usually watch out for them. I take another road home. And normally even if they do see me, they don't catch me. They're rubbish at hiding and I can usually outrun them. But sometimes you just can't avoid them. It's like when you're running across the park and you know there's going to be a big soft dog turd there and you watch out for it, try to avoid it, but there's always that one time when you step right in it. That's what happened the night before the match. I turned a corner and there they were.

I'm usually good at not getting caught. I'm a good runner and I'm wiry with it. I can slip in and out of places the Zombie Bissett brothers get stuck in.

But that night I got caught. I slipped as I was hurtling round a corner, tried to get to my feet. Too late. They were both on me. One grabbed me by the collar, the other hauled me to my feet by the throat. It's scary being caught by the Bissett Boys. They're ugly and they're stupid but they've got a punch like a hammer, and the last time they caught me I ended up with two black eyes.

It's easy to say fight back. But how do you fight back when they're built like sumo wrestlers and there's only one of me – a wee one of me?

It's easy to say tell on them. But remember:

SHARKEY IS A GRASS

You don't grass here – on anybody.

They began to drag me round the back of the shops – obviously didn't want any witnesses – and I was having none of that. Back of the shops? Isolated? Anything could happen. And big Bernie Bissett was cracking his knuckles as if he meant business.

'You are in for it noo, wee man,' he kept saying. He was obviously the one using the brain cell tonight.

He spoke like a real hard man, which as he had me by the throat at that point, he was. Hard as nails. If I disappeared round the back of those shops it was a foregone conclusion that I'd disappear for ever.

So I lashed out with my foot. One sharp kick and I caught big Bernie right on the shin. It was tears-running-down-the-face time for him – running down the legs as well, I hoped. Bernie let out a scream like a lassie. He jumped and grabbed his leg – and fell over.

Honestly, it would have been funny if I hadn't been so scared. But I took the chance to jerk myself free of Bernie's brother, Brian, who was holding my arms. Not quick enough, for Brian's foot shot out and this time it was me who buckled in pain. But it didn't stop me running. If I stumbled they'd get me. So I ran, pain searing through my leg. I bit my lip to keep from shouting. My leg had to be broken, I was sure of it. Let's face it, no one can say my life isn't exciting. It's like living in a gangster movie sometimes.

When I got home I had to hide the pain – and the massive bruise on my shin. Dad and Mum would want to know what happened and I couldn't tell them, because Dad would want to do the right thing, go straight to the police, get them to warn the Bissett Boys off. Or maybe he'd go to the Bissett house, talk to their parents. Then, it would be the Bissetts who would get the police on us, for harassment probably. This family were in trouble so often they had their own personal lawyer.

My dad was one of the good guys. Thought because he obeyed the rules, everybody else did too. Sometimes it was my dad who needed protecting.

So I lied. I'd fallen, I told him.

It was only next day when we were being picked for the team for the final that it really hit me. I couldn't run as fast. I limped when I should have leaped, and I ended up as a last resort reserve.

I told Sean what had happened of course. I told him everything – well, almost everything – and he understood. Still had to make a joke of it.

'You must be kicking yourself, Leo old pal. Oh, wait a minute, I forgot, the Bissett Boys did that for you!'

'I'd love to get them back for this,' I told him.

'Let's see, Leo,' Sean said thoughtfully, tapping his teeth with his finger. 'Revenge on the Bissett Boys? Or staying alive? Difficult decision, eh?'

And he was right. This was the real world, and Sean and I knew it. We were streetwise, me and Sean. I was annoyed that I'd missed playing in the final – but there was no good crying over it. These things happened. It was best just to get on with it. And to be truthful, I was more worried that the Bissett Boys would be determined to get back at *me*.

6

I kept well out of the way of the Bissett Boys for the next couple of days.

That was the easy bit. I usually knew how to avoid them, and I usually succeeded.

But I had other things on my mind. My dad was going through a bad time. Another knock-back for a job. And this one he'd been certain he would get. I'd lost count of the interviews he'd gone for. But he'd been so sure he'd get this one. It was a job in a big electronics firm. He'd been for three interviews, and they had whittled it down to the last two candidates. My dad and some other guy. It would have got him back into electronics. Permanent job, good money, a pension. All he wanted. And when the envelope came through the door that morning, it was obvious he knew what it was. They would have phoned if he'd landed the job. I could see he wanted to just push it back through the letterbox again.

'I'm a real loser,' he said when he finally ripped open the envelope, read the letter inside.

But my dad wasn't a loser. He'd get a job, I knew he would. He wasn't in the mood to listen to any of that. The atmosphere in the house was so bleak. Even David couldn't cheer him up. So when Sean suggested I go back to his house after school that night to play Zombie Doom, I jumped at the chance. Anything not to have to go home.

I phoned Mum on my mobile and she was all for it. 'You have a nice time. Dad'll come and pick you up later.'

Zombie Doom was brilliant. And Sean's mum made us popcorn and tablet. I loved Mrs Brady. She believed a boy couldn't have too much sugar. It was a night to remember. We played so long we forgot the time, until I looked at my watch and realised Dad hadn't come for me yet. I called my mum.

'I was just about to call you.' Her voice was a whisper. 'Any chance of Sean's dad bringing you home?'

I was just about to tell her that Sean's dad was working late tonight when I thought to ask her.

'Why? Where's dad?'

She kept her voice low. David must be in bed sound asleep and she wouldn't want to wake him. 'Och, your dad's been so down today, I told him to go out for a game of snooker with his mates.'

Good idea, I thought, just what Dad needed, but it meant that Dad couldn't collect me, Sean's dad couldn't take me, and Mrs Brady couldn't drive. If I admitted all that to Mum she'd lift David out of bed to come and get me.

So I lied.

If Dad had got the job. If Sean's dad hadn't been working late. If his mum could drive. If I hadn't gone to their house. So many ifs. If any of these things had been different, I wouldn't have walked home alone that night.

But I did.

And changed my life.

7

I lied to Sean's mum too. Told her my dad was picking me up at the corner. Sean knew the truth and backed me to the hilt.

'I don't know why they think we've got to be picked up and dropped off everywhere anyway. We're not parcels.'

But at the door he had a warning for me. 'Sure you'll be able to avoid the Bissett Boys?'

'I know how to miss them. I'm going up over the Larkshill Road. Catch the bus from there.'

It's funny looking back over that night. How so many things led to what happened. Here was another – if I hadn't tried to avoid the Bissett Boys I would have caught another bus home, wouldn't have taken the Larkshill Road. I remember reading a poem once.

Can't remember anything about it except one line –

'Ten out of ten means you are dead.' That night I scored ten out of ten.

I left Sean's and walked up behind the old railway station. Beyond that I was in the estate known as Larkshill. Sounds beautiful, doesn't it? Larkshill. It used to be a dump but now it has sprouted new-build houses. Some of the old ones have been refurbished, trees have been planted. There's a playground in the middle. Now the scheme looks great. It looks now the way it sounds. Larkshill.

Sean's dad and mine always say it should be an estate to be proud of, if they could just get rid of McCrae – the gang boss who ran the whole place – with his money-lending, his drugs, his protection racket. This was still McCrae's turf. He lived round here somewhere, but I didn't know where.

I was only two streets away from the bus stop. Only two streets. Already, I could see the lights of the bus heading towards town. If I ran I might just catch this one. But I'd need a bit of energy for that. I put my hand in my pocket and pulled out my bag of Mint Imperials.

One of them was halfway to my mouth when I heard the click. A sound I'd never heard before, yet a sound that seemed so familiar.

I looked around. The street was in darkness, quiet and empty. All the blinds were drawn, curtains closed.

Then I saw a movement. There was a man standing at the top of a flight of steps that led to someone's front door. He held something in his hand. At first I thought it was a fishing rod, or even a baseball bat. Baseball bats are lethal weapons round here. Even my dad has one behind the front door for protection, just in case. Even though he hates the need for it.

The man's face was in shadow. I saw him rap at the front door and then he moved back and I knew right away what he was doing. He was moving out of the line of sight of the spyhole in the door.

He didn't want whoever opened that door to see him.

I wanted to move. Wanted away from there. Couldn't budge. Feet glued to the ground.

Something was about to happen. Something bad.

I held my breath. My eyes were drawn to the baseball bat. I saw the man raise it waist-high, ready to use it. Even from this distance I was sure I could hear the measured footsteps of someone walking down the hall-way. Hear the chain being drawn across. The handle turning. I couldn't breathe though I wanted to call out and warn whoever it was on the other side of that door.

My voice was like a rock in my throat.

The door opened. A shaft of yellow light let me see more clearly the man waiting outside. A big, solid man, straight backed, and it was then I saw that it wasn't a baseball bat he had in his hands at all but something much more lethal.

It was a shotgun.

Everything seemed to go into slow motion, and yet at the same time move so fast. The man inside the house – I hardly saw him. He stepped back out of sight in the split second he recognised the man on the steps and saw what he was holding. He wasn't quick enough. The shotgun was lifted and there was a sudden blast like thunder, like lightning, yet like no sound I'd ever heard before. The man stumbled back and sparks flew from his body. At least, at first I thought they were sparks, and then in a second I saw what it was.

Blood.

Blood, spraying. Drops of blood glowing like rubies in the streetlight. It sprayed across the gunman, and I saw how he lifted his hand, wiped the blood away that was spattered on his face, spat on his hands in disgust before folding his fingers round the barrel of the gun again.

It was way too much like a movie. It couldn't be real. This was my home town, not the mean streets of New York. If I could just switch it off, change the channel, delete the programme . . .

My hands were shaking so much, the bag of mints began to tremble in my hand. I couldn't hold them. One by one they tumbled to the ground. Hitting the pavement with the rat-a-tat-tat of a machine gun.

Betraying me.

Giving away my position.

The man with the shotgun turned at the sound. For the first time I saw his face clearly in the light from the hallway.

It was Armour.

8

Armour. I had seen him once striding along a street in town as if it was his. As if he owned it.

'The Man', they called him. He was tall and broad and his face seemed etched in stone. He turned that stony face to me now. I wanted to dart back into the darkness but I couldn't move. It was as if my feet were welded to the ground. I held my breath and the world seemed to be switched to silent mode.

Armour's eyes homed in on me. I waited for the shotgun to be raised again, aimed at me. I waited for it. Expected it.

Surely someone would save me? Someone else must have heard the shot? Windows would be thrown open any second now. A voice would shriek at him. He would have to run.

Why were there no people rushing from their houses?

In the second I asked these questions, I answered them myself.

Because it was Armour, and they would all know the shot had come from McCrae's house. It was safer to sit tight and ignore the sound – for even the twitching of a curtain, a slat raised a millimetre on a blind, would mean someone in that house had witnessed it. No one would be safe then. So much more sensible to just turn the volume of the television up a notch. Pretend to have heard nothing.

Better to stay hidden.

But I had nowhere to hide.

Couldn't anyway. For his eyes never left mine.

And then his arm moved. He raised his hand. But the gun stayed where it was. He raised his hand, lifted it to his mouth and drew his fingers along his lips as if he was closing a zip.

Keep your mouth shut. That's what he was telling me.

And then he did something that took me totally by surprise.

He winked.

And as he winked, he smiled. A slow, dark smile that scared me almost as much as the gunshot.

Only then did I back into the shadows. He couldn't

see me. I wasn't important.

He probably thought I was already rushing away from the scene. Glad just to be alive. Because he knew he was safe.

That one gesture was a warning he knew I would heed.

Keep your mouth shut.

Zip your lip.

Yet even then, frightened as I was, I didn't run. I tried to. Tried to step back, but my feet wouldn't move. My legs were like concrete blocks embedded into the ground. I could see him through the bushes, couldn't help but see him, couldn't stop myself watching.

Armour vaulted over the railings outside the front door, landing softly on the grass verge. He stayed low and a shaft of moonlight caught the grey metal of the gun. I almost lost sight of him as he merged into the darkness, but a moment later there he was across the street, heading for the back of one of the derelict shops tucked in the corner.

It was only then my legs obeyed me and moved. The sensible thing to do would have been to run in the opposite direction, get as far away from there as possible. Why couldn't I ever do the sensible thing?

Because instead of running away I found I was moving silently after him, staying behind the cover of the bushes until I could see him, lying belly down close behind the wall of the old deserted Chinese takeaway.

What was he doing?

From here, no one could see him. Not from the houses, not from the street. Only I could see him.

Only me.

He pulled a black bin bag from his pocket and I watched him slide the gun inside it. I knew then what he intended. He was going to hide the gun.

Even Armour wouldn't want to be caught hurrying home carrying a firearm, especially a recently fired one. He couldn't throw it in the river. He wasn't close enough.

So where *was* he going to hide it?

Could he be burying it? But where? It wouldn't be safe to bury it here. The police would search all around this area. And they'd spot newly turned-over earth a mile off. They'd dig the place up for sure. I edged closer to get a better view, couldn't stop myself. I was practically crawling too. And I saw then exactly what he was doing. Not burying it at all. He was sliding the black bag deep, deep, down inside one of the rusty old exposed pipes. His arm almost disappeared up to his shoulder, he thrust it so deep. Then I watched as he stuffed more papers down there too – crisp packets, bits of newspaper that lay around – until the pipe itself was hidden from view. It was a good place to choose. Even if they found the pipe and thought to look there, anyone peering inside would never see the gun. It would be safe until he had the opportunity to retrieve it.

I rolled back against the wall as Armour got to his feet. He looked around once more. His eyes would be alert, watching for anyone who might have seen him. I prayed this time he wouldn't spot me. He dusted himself down and in a few sprints he was gone.

Was it only then someone screamed? Or had they been screaming all along and I'd been deaf to it?

I heard it now. A wailing, tormented scream. Someone at last had found the body lying in the hallway. Windows were opened, lights came on. The street exploded into life. Safe for anyone now to appear and say in all honesty they had seen nothing. Armour was gone.

But not safe for me.

I began to run as if the devil himself was after me. I can't even remember getting the bus. Did I run all the way home? I don't know. It's all a blur, like a nightmare. That journey home, slamming my way into the house. My mum complaining she was trying to watch her favourite programme. I even had some vague conversation with her.

How did I do that? I don't know. It was as if I was on autopilot. Trying to appear normal, yet inside shaking, screaming, desperate to tell someone.

But who could I ever tell?

Too much information is a dangerous thing.

There was no one I could tell. No one.

I dreamed that night. Terrible dreams. Armour kicking down the front door, Terminator-style, coming in through the house, blasting his way into every room. Shooting my mum and dad in their bed. And David . . . I blotted out that part of the nightmare. I couldn't even in a dream bear to think of him being hurt.

And then Armour was coming for me.

I must have cried out, because I woke up with my mum shaking me and cold sweat dripping from my brow.

'That was some nightmare,' she was saying. 'That's the last of these Zombie games for you, boy.'

I was so relieved it was only a dream I almost kissed

her. And then wee David pushed past her, climbed into bed beside me.

'Want to sleep with Leo,' he said. 'I had a nightmare too,' he lied. He always wanted everything I had.

I was glad he was there. He comforted me much more than I comforted him.

'Tell me a story,' he said, when Mum had left us and the light was out. I knew the kind of story he wanted. The kind he always wanted. He and I were superheroes saving the good people from the bad guys.

But I wasn't a superhero – I had brought the bad guys right into the house, putting him in danger.

He was asleep before the story finished, his eyelids fluttering, his wee mouth open. He looked so cute.

'Please,' I prayed. 'Don't let anything bad happen to him because of me.'

9

I didn't feel any better next morning. When I woke up I prayed it had only been part of the nightmare. It hadn't really happened. It couldn't have really happened. Things like this didn't happen to boys like me.

But I knew it was true as soon as I stepped into the kitchen for my breakfast. It was already all round the town. Someone had phoned my dad and told him. It was all he could talk about.

'People getting shot on their doorstep. What kind of place is this turning into?'

Shot on their doorstep . . . I felt the sick rise in my throat when he said that. The memory flooding over me.

'It was only McCrae,' my mum said. I knew she was trying to shut him up, calm him down. But this was my dad. Nothing would shut him up.

'Anybody could have been caught in that crossfire. Look at that poor boy down south, coming home from football on his bike, the life blasted out of him just because he was in the wrong place in the wrong time.'

He turned his eyes on me. I knew what he was thinking. He was imagining it was me on my bike, caught between two rival gangs. Yesterday it would have excited me. I would have imagined the Hollywood version. With stunts and phoney blood and guts all over the place. But not now. Not after last night.

I saw again the blood spraying over Armour's face, and this time I really was sick. Couldn't keep it down.

'I think he's got a bug,' my mum said. She felt my brow. 'He's burning up.'

'Get him back into bed then,' my dad said. 'Keep him off school. I'm here to look after him.'

David leaped in his chair. 'I want to stay off school too. I've got a bug.'

My dad smiled at him. 'No chance, wee man. Anyway, Mrs Bates would cry if her favourite boy didn't come to school.'

Mrs Bates was his teacher and David adored her. He looked from me to the table. Thinking hard. Weighing up our merits. Mrs Bates won.

'OK, I'll go to school.'

I wished I'd won. That he would stay with me. I didn't want him out of my sight.

Was Armour watching the house? Had he found out where I lived? I began to feel sick again.

I was back in bed when Sean phoned me. 'You're not coming to school? Lucky you! What's wrong?'

I so wanted to tell him. Needed someone to tell. But whoever I told would be in danger too.

Maybe I would go to confession this Saturday, tell the priest. He'd be safe and he couldn't tell anyone.

I even saw myself enter the confessional box, kneel down, begin to speak softly through the mesh on the little window between us. Then in my imagination the priest wasn't a priest at all. Father Logan was lying dead somewhere and the man I was confessing to was Armour.

'Hey, pal, are you still there?' Sean bellowed in my ear, brought me back to the present.

'Sorry, I don't feel well,' I said.

'Hey, did you hear what happened last night? McCrae was shot on his doorstep. My dad's up in arms. So's yours. Everybody knows who did it – either Nelis or Armour. But they'll get off with it, my dad says. No witnesses, as usual.' I heard the bell in the background. 'Better go, pal. Phone you later.'

Sean sounded excited. The way I would have done any other time. A shooting on the doorstep – it was like something out of a movie.

Yet his words cheered me up. Everybody knows who did it. Armour would be arrested soon. Why was I so worried? I'd seen it, but so must lots of other people. Scared people peeking through blinds, or out of darkened windows.

Armour would be arrested soon, and it would have nothing to do with me.

I felt so much better I went with Dad to collect David from school. He came running out, shirt hanging out of his trousers, dragging his rucksack behind him. He was clutching a drawing. It was of me and him.

'Have I got wings?' I asked him when he was in the car.

He tutted. 'It's your cloak. You're a superhero.'

'And what's my special power?'

He didn't hesitate. He had obviously thought today's special power through thoroughly. 'You can put out fires with your eyes – like this.'

His eyes went wide and started rolling around in his

head. I copied him exactly.

'Like this?'

My dad was laughing.

'I'm Fireboy, and you're Fireman,' David informed me.

'Look for fires on the way home,' my dad said, laughing. 'Fireman and Fireboy are on their way!'

But it wasn't fires we saw on the way home. It was something much more ominous – just round the corner from our house, a whitewashed message that couldn't be missed.

GRASSES DIE HERE

10

It was meant for me. It had to be meant for me. I was sure of it. A warning. That writing hadn't been there yesterday. I would have spotted it. Couldn't have missed it. Those giant whitewashed letters.

GRASSES DIE HERE

As soon as we got in the door I was sick again.

'I think I should call the doctor,' my mum said.

'Don't be daft. He's only got a wee bug. Let his body fight it off itself.'

That was always my dad's opinion. Fight it off yourself. Don't rely on pills.

He was right. I didn't need an antibiotic. All I needed was to know that Armour had been arrested or that he'd forgotten all about me.

Sean was on the phone later that night with his exciting news and that only made things worse for me. 'Cops are just away. Asking questions. They're going round all the doors about here. "Did we see anything suspicious."' Then he laughed. 'Up here? We see something suspicious every day. You should have heard my dad. "What are you going round the houses for? Everybody knows you've only got two suspects . . . Armour and Nelis."' Sean did a great impression of his dad's gruff voice. He almost had me laughing.

'Is that what everybody thinks?' I knew they did but I had to have the reassurance.

'Course they do. They even asked us if we'd seen any of them last night.'

'Would you have told them if you had?'

He let out a bellyful of laughter. 'Are you kiddin', Leo? I like living. We're keeping our mouths shut. As long as they're only killing each other, that's what my dad says.'

That was better than an antibiotic. Sean wouldn't tell either. He'd keep his mouth shut too. And he was right. Armour had only shot McCrae, not some poor innocent guy who didn't deserve it.

'Hey, Leo, I'm just thinking. You must have been on

your way home when the shooting happened. Did you see anything suspicious?'

Now was the perfect time to blurt out the truth to my mate. Swear him to secrecy. Sean would never break a promise, and I would have someone to talk to about it.

Yet in the same second I remembered those letters again, written on the wall.

GRASSES DIE HERE

If I told Sean he might – without thinking, without meaning to – one day let something slip to his dad. We would all be in danger then.

Where did the lie come from? And when did I learn to lie so easily?

'I was well on the way home when that must have happened. On the bus. Only suspicious thing I saw was some guy paying his fare with foreign money.'

I almost believed it myself.

The knot in my stomach disappeared after Sean's call. I felt better. I'd done the right thing not telling him. Sean was my mate. I couldn't put him in danger just because I needed someone to talk to. Armour by now would know I wasn't going to grass him up. His secret was safe with me. He'd forget about me.

I went back to school next day. Miracle recovery, my dad told me. My mum said it had been a twenty-four-hour bug and she hoped David didn't get it. In answer David ran into the downstairs toilet and pretended to be sick. Told you he always wants what I've got.

Over the next couple of days I almost forgot about the shooting. I even stopped having nightmares about it. It became almost like a scary movie I'd seen – not real at all.

Then one night I woke up. Cold sweat. My first thought.

Mint Imperials.

My Mint Imperials. I had left them at the scene of the crime. Not one. Not two. But the whole blinking bag of them. They had betrayed me the night of the shooting. They could betray me again.

The police were looking for witnesses. They would find my mints. If they were doing their job properly they *should* have found them.

Everyone knew how much I loved my Mint Imperials. I imagined someone mentioning that to the cops.

'I know a boy – sell his soul for a Mint Imperial. Leo McCabe.' Then they would take the mints to forensics. My fingerprints would be on them, my DNA. They would trace them back to me.

I heard a car in the distance, coming closer. Heading for my house, I was sure. I held my breath . . . but the car passed on another road. The sound faded into the distance.

It wasn't the police. Not this time. But it would be. I'd seen enough cop shows to know you couldn't escape. They'd find me.

They always find you.

Those Mint Imperials were going to be the death of me.

And I fell back to sleep eventually thinking, my mum was right. She is always warning me that sweets aren't good for you.

Things went back to a kind of normality. Sean came to my house for his tea and I even went to his. No risk there. Dad picked me up and we went nowhere near McCrae's house. Couldn't get near it anyway.

'Police have got it cordoned off,' my dad said.

And for a second I remembered Armour and the

blood and the gun.

And Veronika Kuschinska smiled at me.

Did I say that? I don't care whether she smiles at me or not. I only try to be nice to her because she's new here. But Sean insisted I blushed all over when she smiled. 'Even your spots blushed,' he said.

'I did not! You're winding me up. I must have a rash from that bug I had.'

Maybe I was still blushing when I walked home from school that day. I certainly wasn't concentrating. I must try to be cool, that's what I was thinking. And blushing in front of a lassie just isn't cool.

I turned the corner and walked right into the Bissett Boys.

They were standing in front of me, blocking my path. There was no way they could miss seeing me. My mind immediately started to work out an escape route – back the way I'd come or over the wall and through the back greens of the tenements.

I held my breath because I knew they were too close. They turned when they heard my footsteps behind them. Too close. They could reach out and grab me from here. I wouldn't have time to run. I began to panic.

And do you know what happened?

They were the ones who stepped back from me.

Both of them.

They saw me and moved back and there was something in their eyes I couldn't understand. They didn't say a word to each other, as if they had talked together about what they would do already, knew in advance what they would do if they saw me. They just took a few steps away from me and without saying a word they broke into a run and left me.

Puzzled.

Amazed.

The Bissett Boys had had a chance to pulverise me – to break me into little pieces – and they'd run off instead.

Maybe they'd decided to turn over a new leaf.

Maybe they'd found religion.

Maybe they'd left the family brain cell at home.

I hurried home myself in case they changed their minds. And it was only as I closed my front door behind me that I realised what the look in their eyes had been.

Fear.

11

Why would the Bissett Boys leave me alone? They'd
never done that before. I had always been an easy target
for them. They'd been bold enough to follow me to my
door, even though they knew my mum and dad would be
there.

Now, tonight, they had stepped away from me,
turned their backs on me and looked at me with something in their eyes I was sure had been fear.

I must be mistaken.

I mean, how would I know what fear in their eyes
would look like?

Yet they had turned away from me as if they were
afraid.

I was sure I was right. They were scared of me.

I was desperate to tell Sean this new development, see
what he thought.

What stopped me? Because I didn't call him, didn't even tell him next day at school. And he knew I was holding something back.

'What is wrong with you, Leo?' he asked.

I wanted to tell him, even began babbling something to him. But I found the words just wouldn't come.

'You're in a dream. Have you got something on your mind?'

I didn't have to answer him.

Sean supplied the answer himself. 'Dreaming of Veronika, is that it?'

At that moment Veronika had just walked by. A couple of other girls had made friends with her. She was arm in arm with them, smiling at something they were saying. The other two began to giggle but Veronika still only smiled. Like that Mona Lisa lassie. Did she understand what they were saying? Her English was really good – almost perfect in fact. She probably spoke better English than me. But she did sometimes miss a joke, didn't quite get our humour.

My eyes followed her.

Sean watched me. He laughed, put his arm round my shoulder. 'Aye, it's Veronika,' he said. Satisfied he was right.

Let him think it *was* Veronika who was on my mind. I could never tell him who it really was.

Every time there was a knock on the door, every time the phone rang, my heart stopped. My mind was in constant turmoil, as if it was caught in a twister. Going from graffiti on a wall to Mint Imperials and now to the Bissett Boys.

And still the gossip round the town was all about the shooting. Headlines about it in the local paper every night.

I'M GLAD HE'S DEAD

Mr Sheridan, the man whose daughter had died, was never out of the paper. He had hated McCrae with a vengeance for what he'd done to his daughter.

Nelis's photo was in the paper too. Emerging from the police station sneering, holding up his hand in a victory salute.

THEY'VE GOT NOTHING ON ME

Those were the words he'd spoken after being taken

in for questioning.

And Armour. I froze when I saw his photo staring at me from the front page. Couldn't help reading the story. He had a cast-iron alibi, the paper reported.

'Surprise, surprise,' my dad said when he read it. 'He's probably got a few cast-iron alibis lined up.'

But there were still no leads.

'Someone knows something,' a police spokesman was reported as saying. 'But they're too afraid to come forward. They have no reason to be afraid. We will protect them. Be sure of it.'

Aye, right! The police must know that was rubbish. They couldn't protect you. If I came forward, I'd be a dead man or my whole family would have to go on the witness protection programme. We would have to hide for ever. Change identities. No way.

Sean came home with me one night after school and my dad was reading the evening paper. 'Look at this!' he said, showing us another headline.

VICTIM WAS LIKE A FATHER TO US

His finger almost went through the page. 'People in that street are saying McCrae was like a father to them. A man they could all rely on. He made them feel safe. Children were in and out of his house all day, for advice. For help.'

Sean laughed. 'For drugs.'

My dad nodded grimly. 'Aye, probably for drugs.'

'What makes them say things like that, Mr McCabe?' Sean asked.

'They're scared of him,' my dad said. 'He's dead and they're still scared of him.'

'Well, my dad says at least now he's dead the place is free of him.'

But my dad didn't agree with that.

'No. The other two will be fighting over his territory – just wait. There'll be more violence.'

Sean loved the idea of that. He pushed me into my room. 'Gang warfare! Exciting, isn't it? It's like living inside one of our computer games.'

But I couldn't get excited about it the way I would have done just a few days ago. Because I'd seen McCrae's blood spraying out over that doorstep. Real blood. Real death. Too real.

This wasn't a game. It was real life. And I was in the middle of it.

Would I ever stop feeling like this? I woke up every

morning thinking this time it would fade. The memory would fade. I would put it behind me. But something always happened to bring it right back at me. And Sean saw the difference in me.

'You need cheering up, son. You've been a bit down lately,' he said, as if he was my old grandad. 'Who says we'll go into town on Saturday and get ourselves a new game?'

It sounded good to me. What would I do without Sean? I met him at the bus stop and we spent ages choosing exactly the right game – yet another Zombie game. Zombie Flesh-eaters this time. Then we went for a burger. It was late afternoon and we were walking through the mall, laughing and looking forward to a Saturday night with the Zombies, when I saw him.

Armour.

If I'd noticed him sooner I would have pulled Sean into one of the shops. Avoided him completely. But I saw him too late. He was almost on us. Striding through the mall as if he owned it. His nickname came back to me. He was The Man, and at that moment he looked the part. He was flanked by two of his henchmen. Big hard-looking guys, like a couple of sumo wrestlers.

My mouth went so dry my lips stuck together. I

prayed he wouldn't notice me. I tried not to look at him. Kept my own eyes glued to the ground.

It was his shoes I saw coming closer – his shiny leather shoes. He would walk past me in a moment, probably hadn't even seen me anyway. That's what I kept telling myself.

Yet at that last moment I had to look. Couldn't stop myself. My eyes were drawn to his. And just when I was sure he hadn't even noticed me, he looked straight at me. He smiled.

And then, he winked.

12

He was past me in a moment. I didn't look back. My eyes immediately darted to Sean but he had noticed nothing. Too taken up with the PlayStations in W. H. Smith's window. I don't think he even noticed Armour coming towards us anyway.

Armour had winked at me. With that smile on his face, a smile that said he was . . . pleased with me. A wink that said 'Thanks'. For keeping quiet. For not saying a word. For zipping my lip.

I walked taller along the mall. I know I did. Shoulders back, my spine straight, striding forward, like a soldier.

I felt . . . dead chuffed.

I felt . . . good.

The fear seemed to drop from my shoulders like a wet coat.

It was at that moment I knew I had done the right

thing. I had protected myself, and my family. Armour wouldn't come blasting his way into my house. That friendly wink had proved it.

I had done the right thing not telling Sean as well. He would have given it all away when he saw Armour walking towards us. Without wanting to, without even realising it, Sean would have given himself away.

I had protected him too.

And anyway, why *should* I tell? Wasn't everyone saying they were only killing each other? Armour had shot one of the bad guys. One less in the town.

'You're talking to yourself, do you know that, pal?' Sean pulled me round.

Had I been talking to myself?

'And you've got a big stupid grin on your face.'

'Me?'

'Dreaming of Veronika, are you?'

Veronika, with her long blonde hair and her sea-green eyes. I didn't argue with him. Better he thought I was thinking of her than know the truth.

'Well, you'd better get in there quick, 'cause I heard that Aidan Shaw fancies her as well.'

'Big lanky Aidan Shaw?' I said. 'He doesn't stand a chance next to me.'

That night I thrashed Sean at Zombie Flesh-eaters. We had a great night at his house. His mum made her speciality spag bol, and Dad came to collect me with David in tow.

We had a ball on the way home, playing soldiers in the back seat of the car and then superheroes when we got back home.

I had a dreamless, contented sleep that night. First time since . . . The incident.

And on Monday things only got better.

My dad got a job.

I'd never seen him smile so wide. He waved the letter in my face as soon as I stepped into the kitchen for my breakfast. 'Your dad's got a job!'

He lifted David high in the air and swung him round. My mum looked so happy too. A big daft grin on her face. A moment to remember.

'It's not a great job,' he told us over breakfast. 'It's just labouring work at the building site. Seems some guy I know suggested me to the foreman. But I always say once you've got a job it's easier to get another.'

When I went to school Sean knew all about it too. My dad had phoned his dad as soon as he got the letter.

'Things are definitely getting better, eh?'

My dad came to collect me after school. David was with him. 'We're all going out for a celebration tea. I'm collecting your mum at the hospital.'

'Not even got a wage yet and you're spending all the money, eh?'

My dad laughed. 'It's OK, your mum's paying . . . but don't tell her yet.'

It was a great day all round.

Veronika even smiled at me – not that that was important. Forget I said it.

But as I lay in bed that night, listening to my mum and dad talking and laughing and making plans downstairs – the way I hadn't heard them in a long time – I don't think I'd ever felt so happy.

The only dark spot was those mints. Were they even now in some forensic laboratory being studied, dusted for prints, being discussed as a possible clue to the murder?

The very thought of it made me want to vomit.

I wiped the thought away. I was just being silly. They wouldn't be interested in my Mint Imperials. I was safe.

Things would have been so different if I'd confessed to what I'd seen. We'd be on the witness protection programme. We'd all be in danger. We'd probably have to change identities, move somewhere else. I wouldn't be lying here in my own bed, and my dad wouldn't be starting his new job next week.

No. I had definitely done the right thing.

13

The same week my dad got the job McCrae had his funeral. It was Sean who urged me to go. I didn't want to. I knew my mum and dad would want me to keep well back from it – and I also knew it would bring back too many horrible memories.

But Sean wouldn't let it go. 'It's going to be pure show business, Leo. You know the drug dealers and the gang bosses always have the best funerals.'

And he was right. Their funerals were like royal events.

He saw I was still hesitating and he wondered why. I never had before. 'What has been wrong with you lately? You're acting weird.' And once again he came up with the same answer and I let him believe it. 'Veronika,' he said. 'It's because you saw big Aidan talking to her, isn't it?'

I hadn't actually seen that at all. Aidan Shaw? What could Veronika possibly see in him? He was tall and skinny with sticky-out teeth like a horse and half the girls in the school drooled over him. I'll never understand women. Would Veronika fancy him too?

Sean answered the question I hadn't even asked. 'I don't think she even likes him. She kept looking over at you when he was talking to her.'

'Did she?' That surprised me. Could Veronika possibly be interested in me?

Sean nudged me and laughed. 'See I *knew* it was her that was putting you in a dream. I see her sneaking a look at you all the time.'

'Seems to me you spend more time looking at Veronika than I do.'

But still he went on and on about this funeral. It was to take place on Saturday morning and a big crowd was expected. Who would want to go to see McCrae's funeral, I wondered.

But a lot of people did.

And in the end, I was one of them. I ran out of excuses for Sean and I was dragged there reluctantly.

We could hardly find a place to stand just to watch. The streets leading from the funeral parlour to the cemetery were lined with people.

'Why are so many people here?' I said to Sean.

'To make sure he's dead,' Sean said without a bit of hesitation. 'McCrae tries to climb out of that coffin and a hundred people will whip out their sub-machine guns and shoot him again.'

The thought made me feel sick. I had seen him die once. Didn't want to see it again.

Sean found a great spot for us to watch the parade – sorry, funeral – a lamp post near the cemetery gates we could both step up on and which would give us a clear view of the street. I still wondered why all these people had come to watch the final passing of an arch villain. Was it to see the spectacle? Or was it really to reassure themselves that he had gone for good?

It certainly wouldn't be out of respect.

Everyone knew McCrae had been responsible for beatings, for selling drugs outside schools, for shootings. No one could forget the Sheridan girl. He had got off with her murder too. But everyone knew he was guilty. No doubt about that.

No, people surely hadn't come here out of respect.

Sean tapped my arm. 'Hear that? They're coming.'

At first I couldn't make out the sound. Then I realised

it was the clip-clip of horses' hooves. The crowd fell silent.

The procession turned the corner. It was led by a young boy in a tall black hat and a frock coat. He walked solemnly in front of a glass coach pulled by four jet-black horses. The black plumes on their heads quivered in the breeze. McCrae's coffin lay in the back in full view, even though the carriage was filled with all kinds of floral tributes.

THE BEST DAD IN THE WORLD

McCrae had several children all by different mothers and seldom saw any of them.

OUR BEST FRIEND

That was another joke. McCrae had no friends. People feared him too much to become his friend.

Sean was thoroughly enjoying the whole spectacle. 'Hey! Can you read that one, Leo?' He pointed it out to me. A great wreath of red and white roses.

SADLY MISSED.

* * *

He tried to stifle his laugh. 'He wasn't missed though, was he? Somebody got him, right in the –' Sean grabbed at his chest, pretended to tumble to the ground.

It wasn't like that, I wanted to tell him, remembering the spray of blood. Feeling sick again at the memory of it.

Why had I come here?

After the carriage there was a silent procession of mourners.

McCrae's mother, weeping, held up by two of her daughters, stumbled along at the front. All three were moneylenders, with a reputation for beating people up who couldn't pay on time.

Everyone was in black – a long snake-like column of black following the carriage.

And there, right behind the family, was Armour. He was carrying a wreath. His face was suitably grim. Was he remembering the moment he had shot McCrae? Was he regretting it?

At one point the mother stumbled. She almost fell, and it was Armour who leaned forward and steadied her with one firm hand. She glanced back at him and smiled gratefully.

I wanted to scream at her, 'Don't smile at him. He killed your son!'

But she must have suspected that anyway. There were rumours all through the town that it was either Armour or Nelis who were the prime suspects. Was she afraid too? Afraid of Armour now she had no son to protect her?

Probably.

They walked on, following the glass carriage through the cemetery gates and up the long winding path to the crematorium. The crowds broke up after that.

Sean jumped from the lamp post. 'Told you it would be pure show business.' He wiped his hands. 'Well, that's him gone. Up in smoke. Best way really. Too many people would be scared he'd rise from the dead at midnight and come after them.' He put on his best Zombie face and started chasing me.

I started laughing too. He was right. McCrae was out of the picture. One less villain in town.

And as for Armour, I'd never see him again.

14

'If you don't chat up Veronika today, you're gonnae miss your chance.'

Sean, on Monday, still going on about Veronika. He nodded over to where she stood at the corner of the English department corridor with one of the girls who had made friends with her. Shannon Farrell.

'You think I'm gonnae go over and chat her up with Shannon Farrell there?' Shannon Farrell was the kind of girl who could freeze you with a look at twenty paces. Half the boys in the school were terrified of her. I was one of them. 'And anyway, I don't want to chat her up at all. I don't know why you keep going on about that.'

'Because I'm your best mate and I know exactly what you're thinking.' He leaned towards me and whispered. 'And I know you're thinking about Veronika. And you better stop thinking and start talking before she's taken back to Poland.'

That shook me. 'How? Is she leaving?'

'Heard her dad can't get his work permit renewed or something. So take your chance now, boy!' He grinned from ear to ear. I know people say that all the time but Sean's the only person I know who can actually manage it – grinning from ear to ear. I always tell him it's because he's got a big mouth.

Thinking about Veronika indeed. Just because she's got that long blonde hair, and green eyes like the sea and – I've hardly noticed her, honest. He nudged me so hard I stumbled.

'Go on. Go up to her and offer her a Mint Imperial.'

'Oh great chat-up line. "Fancy a Mint Imperial?"'

'Where are your Mint Imperials anyway? I haven't seen you eating any for ages.'

The sudden thought of them made me feel sick. I hadn't bought them, hadn't wanted one since . . .

Mint Imperials, tumbling out of the bag on to the pavement with a rat-a-tat-tat, like machine-gun fire.

'Are you OK, Leo? You've gone white.'

I tried to grin from ear to ear . . . not got the mouth for it.

'It's the canteen dinner. It's coming back on me.'

Now it was Sean's turn to go white. 'Canteen dinners!' He pretended to choke. 'They should use them instead of weapons of mass destruction.' He looked across at Veronika. 'Aw, look at that. You've missed your chance again. Look who's chatting her up now.'

Aidan Shaw, standing there like a big drip. I could never understand how any girl could fancy him. But he was never short of a girlfriend. Whatever he was saying to Veronika, he was making her laugh. Her teeth seemed to sparkle in the sunshine, bright and white. Not surprising, considering her dad was a dentist. He was even making Shannon laugh. No mean feat. A snarl was usually the nearest thing she got to a smile.

But she was laughing now.

Sean patted my shoulder. 'You know what they say, pal. If you're no' fast, you're last.'

I wandered home that day from school in a bit of a dream. I wasn't thinking of Veronika, I wasn't hearing that laugh of hers. She was the last thing on my mind. No – I was thinking of nothing in particular. Not anything that I can remember now.

And I turned a corner on to a quiet street and there he was.

Armour.

He was leaning against a car, a silver grey Mercedes, and smoking a cigarette. It was as if he hadn't noticed me. But I knew he had.

I almost turned and ran back, out of his sight before he'd even seen me.

If you're not fast . . .

I wasn't fast enough. He turned in that split second I was thinking about it and his blue eyes locked on mine.

I stopped walking. Couldn't move if you'd paid me.

It was Armour who started walking towards me.

Why?

I'd kept my mouth shut. Hadn't told a soul.

I tried to make out if he had a concealed weapon on him. Would I notice it? A bulge in his jacket, a gun hidden up his sleeve ready to be whipped into his hand?

The street was empty. Traffic on the nearby road sounded miles away.

I was alone. Alone on a lonely side street with a killer.

I was the only one who knew his secret. The only witness to his crime.

The only one who could testify against him.

And now he was heading straight at me.

I was a dead man.

15

He stopped right in front of me. I couldn't bring myself to raise my eyes to his. Instead, I concentrated on his brown leather shoes.

'Leo, isn't it?'

My eyes shot up to his face then. He knew my name. He had blue eyes that seemed to bore right through me.

'Do you live around here?' he asked me.

He knew my name – I'd bet he knew exactly where I lived too.

I wanted to ask him what he was doing but my voice had dried up in my throat.

'I'm glad I bumped into you, Leo,' he said. As if it was an accident. As if he hadn't been waiting here on this quiet street just for me. 'I wanted to thank you.'

I began to feel sick again. I didn't want him to thank me for keeping my mouth shut. But it was what he said next that stunned me.

'I hope I already have thanked you . . . in a small way.'

What did he mean by that? He'd already thanked me? 'Wh – what?' The word seemed to stumble out of my mouth, like a drunk man.

'I hope the Bissett Boys haven't been bothering you any more?'

I took a step back. Armour grabbed at my arm as if he thought I would fall, and I almost did.

'You spoke to the Bissett Boys.'

'Well, let's say I had some friends of mine have a word with them.'

The Bissett Boys would never bother me again. I could walk the streets without fear.

'Thanks.' I couldn't help saying it.

He shook his head. He had a mop of thick brown hair and when he shook his head it seemed to move like a wave. 'Don't you go thanking me. You're the one I should be thanking.' He moved against the railings. A slight touch of my sleeve and I moved with him. From this spot no one could see us. This was a quiet, tree-lined street with hardly a passing car.

'It was a terrible thing you witnessed, Leo. A terrible thing. I wanted to explain to you.'

How do you explain cold-blooded murder, I wanted to ask him. But I said nothing. I was still too afraid. But I was surprised too – surprised that he was speaking like this to me. And I was intrigued. Yes, that's the word. Intrigued. I wanted to know what he was going to say next.

'McCrae was scum,' he said. 'Real scum. Sold drugs at school gates. Did you know that?'

Of course I knew that. Almost everyone in my school and everybody else's did. We could see the cars on the street outside the school at lunchtime – McCrae's cars – and pupils leaning in, buying whatever was for sale.

'Have you seen any lately, Leo?'

I didn't even have to think about it. Since McCrae's death the cars no longer appeared.

'I made sure of that,' Armour said. 'That's one thing I'll have nothing to do with.' He took a long final draw on his cigarette, then flicked it over the railings. 'McCrae was out of control. Remember the Sheridan lassie?'

How could anyone forget the Sheridan lassie?

'That was terrible,' Armour went on. 'McCrae wasn't just a hard man. He was evil. And he was getting worse. Getting off with her murder, that was the final straw. I knew then the police would never get him.'

He was right. I had even heard my dad saying the same thing.

'Somebody had to get rid of McCrae. I'm just sorry, really sorry, you had to be there to see it.'

'So am I,' I heard myself say.

'It would be different if it had been an innocent man, Leo. I would have expected you to speak up. But it was McCrae. He was only getting what he deserved.'

Everything he said seemed to make sense. He hadn't meant for me to see, that was pure accident. And McCrae would just have gone on and on with his evil if he – Armour – hadn't stopped him. Armour had done the town a favour.

And I had kept my mouth shut and the Bissett Boys would never be after me again.

I was trying to find a downside in all this, and couldn't.

'Leo,' Armour said, smiling. 'That means lion – the symbol of kings. Did you know that?'

'I'm called after my grandad,' I told him.

'There are so few people in the world you can trust, Leo,' he said. 'Especially in my world. I could use a boy like you. A boy who knows how to keep his mouth shut.'

He held out his hand to me. A big, tanned hand. He had a villa in Spain, I'd heard. And on his finger a gold coin ring. 'The King of Bling', my dad called him. My dad would never give him the dignity of calling him 'The Man'. But I held out my hand, and shook his. I was even more glad now that I'd kept my mouth shut. It was too late anyway to say anything. How could I explain waiting so long to come forward?

'Good lad,' he said. He began to back away, heading again for his car. He'd gone only a few steps when he stopped.

'By the way . . . hope your dad likes his new job.'

16

He got into his car and drove off. Raising his arm in a goodbye wave to me, Leo McCabe. I was alone again on the quiet street before those last words he had said to me sunk in.

'Hope your dad likes his new job.'

He knew my dad had a new job.

How?

Or did he just know everything about me? He knew my name. He had found out about the Bissett Boys, knew my dad was out of work. What else did he know?

I walked on in a kind of dream, and it took me a while to sort it all out in my mind. He had called off the Bissett Boys – his way of thanking me.

My dad had got a job. Was that another of his ways of thanking me? Could he do that? Get my dad a job?

I'd heard my dad say that Armour had a finger in

every pie. Couldn't quite figure out what he meant by that till he explained that he owned legitimate businesses, buying them with dirty money earned from selling drugs and guns, my dad said. It was called money laundering.

Had my dad got a job in one of the businesses he owned?

And even as I thought it, was that such a bad thing?

McCrae was a real bad guy and Armour had disposed of him. Did that make Armour so bad? He could have disposed of me too. I'd been waiting for it. Instead, he had rewarded me.

Had my life got worse because I'd kept quiet?

No. It had got better. I wasn't afraid walking home now. Wouldn't be again. Even if I was to see the Bissett Boys standing in front of me, blocking my way, I wouldn't be afraid.

They would be the ones who'd be afraid.

And I was going home and my dad wouldn't be sitting gloomily watching afternoon television. Instead, he wouldn't be home till teatime. He'd come in smiling, and him and Mum would chat together, laugh together. They would make plans for getting something done in the house or booking a holiday. Things we couldn't afford before. The whole atmosphere in the house was different now he was working again.

And all this because I had kept my lip zipped – my mouth shut. I'd kept quiet.

If only I could have talked it all through with Sean. I would have loved to have phoned him as soon as I got home, told him everything. But all this had happened because I had told no one. Not even Sean. It had to remain my secret.

Did I walk taller when I went to school next day? I thought I did. Sure of myself. Confident. Unafraid. There must have been something different about me because Sean noticed.

'Hey, you look pleased with yourself! Did you win the Lottery or something?'

'Why? Am I grinning from ear to ear?'

'Just about.' He stared at me. 'Hey, wait a minute. Bet I know. You phoned Veronika last night. She said she fancies you. No accounting for taste, is there?'

'Belt up about Veronika,' I told him. And he did, for a wee while at least.

But I was happy that day. My life could only get better after that. I was sure of it.

17

Tuesday was my Scout night. Sean didn't come. He thought the Scouts were rubbish, but I had been a member since the Cubs and I still enjoyed it.

'Sitting around a camp fire singing "Ging-gang-goolie"? I don't think so,' he would say. That was his opinion of the Scouts.

The Scout hut wasn't far from my house, but far enough for my dad or mum always to insist on picking me up. That night, I got a text from my dad.

Workin l8 w8 4 me

He hadn't a clue how to text messages.

Johnny, the Scout leader, told me it would be no bother for me to stay on. 'I've got a couple of things to sort out. You can wait in the office with me.'

That was the plan, until I looked through one of the windows and saw a man standing on the tree-lined street. Armour.

He was waiting for me. Had to be. But why?

And did that mean he knew where I went on a Tuesday night? Did he know everything about me? Did he know my dad was working late?

He'd got my dad the job – maybe he could make sure my dad was kept late so he could come here and talk to me.

Why?

I wanted to ignore him, sit in the office with Johnny. But my curiosity got the better of me. I had to know why he was here.

'I'm going to wait outside, Johnny,' I said, standing up. 'It's a nice night anyway.'

'Sure thing, Leo. But don't go without letting me know your dad's come for you.'

It was a lovely night. The sky was pink, and gave the whole street a pink glow. Even the trees were pink. It gave everything an unreal feeling. As if I was moving into some kind of fantasy world.

The door of the Scout hut closed behind me and I crossed the road to where Armour stood under the trees.

As I was walking towards I said him, 'You knew my dad would be working late. Did you arrange that?'

Armour smiled. He had white, even teeth. He took care of himself. His hair, his clothes, his teeth. He wore expensive clothes. He wore gold.

'Yeah, Murphy, the guy who owns the company – he owes me a favour.'

'Another one? Didn't you use up your favours getting my dad the job in the first place?'

Where did I get the nerve, talking to Armour like that? But I had to know.

'You're a smart boy, Leo,' he said. 'I like that.'

I wanted to tell him I didn't care what he liked, but this time the words just wouldn't come.

'You're wondering why I'm here, I suppose.'

I glanced around, making sure no one could see us together. If my dad found out I was even talking to Armour he'd go spare. I checked the window of the Scout hut in case Johnny was watching. But no one was there.

'It crossed my mind,' I said.

'I need a favour from you, Leo.'

He needed a favour from me, Leo McCabe?

'You're a boy I can trust. You've proved that. There

are so few people I can trust – in fact, there's no one I can trust. Not for this.'

I stepped back. A cold shiver froze my spine. 'I'm not doing anything illegal.' I was regretting even coming out to talk to him. I didn't want to do him any favours.

He shook his head. 'No, Leo. I'd never ask you to do anything like that. I need you to pass a message on for me. Only a message. That's all.'

My heart was pounding. I wished I was anywhere else but here. My common sense told me to bolt. Self-preservation – and curiosity – kept me there.

'You know how bad things are in this town, Leo,' he went on. His voice was soft. 'I want things to get better. I've had enough of violence. It was the way I grew up, Leo. My dad was a hard man.'

And I remembered my dad telling me that. How people were scared of Armour's father. 'Big Bad Armour', they used to call him.

'I thought I had to be a hard man too,' Armour went on. 'But I want to be finished with all that. Can you understand that, Leo? I want to live a decent life. I want my family to live a decent life. And to do that, I have to make peace with Nelis. No more fighting. No more trouble. Now that McCrae's out of the picture, it's time we did that.'

'Can't you just phone him?' I heard myself say.

'Can't trust phones. Phones can be bugged.'

'Email him then.'

He smiled again. 'Email Nelis? I don't think so. No, I have to let him know I want to make a deal with him. But I can't have anyone know what I'm doing till it's done. It has to be top secret. So I need someone I can trust to set it up. I want you to be my go-between. Do you know what a go-between is, Leo?'

'What it says, I suppose. I go between the two of you, passing messages.'

'Would you do that for me – pass a message to Nelis?'

'Have I got a choice?'

'There's always a choice, Leo. It's up to you. I won't hold it against you if you say no.'

He had dealt with the Bissett Boys for me. My dad had a job thanks to him. He was only asking me to do this one little thing. What was the harm in it, I thought. Pass a message. A message that might bring peace to the town. Something my dad was always saying he wanted. A peaceful town again.

There was no time to think it all through. My dad would be here soon. I couldn't let him catch me speaking to Armour.

A decision had to be made.

There's always a choice.

I made mine.

'OK. Where do you want me to meet him?'

18

Armour was gone by the time my dad arrived. When he picked me up he said I looked as if I was in a daze, standing there at the door of the Scout hut waiting for him, gazing off into the sunset. He was right. My head was in another place altogether.

What had I done?

I had wanted to put it all behind me. Be finished with it – Armour out of my life. And here I was promising to go to Nelis, give him Armour's message. Tell Nelis he wanted to make a deal.

I felt sick inside again. I'd felt sick since Armour's car had moved off, swallowed by the trees, reminding me of a silver snake slithering back into the undergrowth.

'Sorry you had to wait, son,' Dad said. 'Last-minute order. Don't know how it couldn't have waited till the morning but I couldn't very well say no. I've only started in the job. Knew you'd be OK here with Johnny.'

And it seemed to me then at that moment, I knew more than my dad. I knew why that order couldn't wait. And I knew that I hadn't been OK.

I thought about it all next day – a dread in my stomach. Couldn't get it out of my mind. I was going to meet Nelis after school.

'He'll be at the pool hall. He practically lives there,' Armour had said. 'Go there and just tell him. I want to make a deal with him. He'll know what I mean.'

That was all. Seemed simple.

I'd told Mum I was going into town after school. I'd told Sean I was going straight home. It was a carefully planned operation. I'd said I would do it, and I would. A payback for my dad's job – and for the Bissett Boys.

And that would be that. Finished.

I did a U-turn after I left school, taking the road into town and hoping no one would see me. Thinking all the time what excuse I would make if they did.

And Armour's message repeating itself over and over in my head: 'I want to make a deal.'

A peace deal. A deal to stop the fighting and bring peace to the town. That thought was all that consoled me. It kept me going. What I was doing might stop all the gang fighting in the town.

The pool hall is on the main road at the far end of the town. They say you take your life in your hands if you play pool in that place. My dad never does. He goes to Barnhill FC's pool hall.

The pool hall is where Nelis and all his boys hung out. He was there, standing on the steps at the front door as I walked towards it. As if he was waiting for me. He watched me as I came near, and as I climbed the steps to the entrance he flicked the cigarette he was smoking over my head on to the pavement. He wanted to scare me. I was glad to say I didn't flinch.

Nelis was skinny, his face scarred by the fights he'd been in. He had a mop of pale red hair. He didn't look half as impressive as Armour. Nelis looked like your typical ned. But he was much scarier. There were loads of stories about him. Like the one about the best friend he had taken up over the moors and put a gun to his head. He'd claimed the friend was stealing from him. As if anyone would dare to steal from Nelis. He took his car, made him strip off, and then told him to get out of town and never come back. That 'friend' had never been seen again. But others weren't so lucky.

Nelis was bad.

I'd never seen him before – not in the flesh. But his photo had been in the papers so often he was easy to recognise. I remembered one photo in particular. Coming out of court sneering at the cameras, two fingers held high. A 'not-proven' verdict for a crime everyone knew he'd committed.

I tried to keep my voice steady. Tried to look him straight in the eye. 'I've brought you a message from Armour.'

He didn't answer me. Just stared at me with watery blue eyes. They weren't a match for the colour of Armour's.

'He said . . . he wants to make a deal.'

His mouth curled. I had a feeling that passed for a smile with Nelis. He nodded. 'A deal, eh?'

'Yes.'

'Sounds OK to me. You tell him we have to meet then.'

I almost tumbled back down the stairs. 'I can't tell him,' I said. 'I'll not be seeing him again.'

'Sure you will,' he said. 'You tell Armour if he wants a deal, we have to meet.'

I wanted to scream at him. This was me finished. No

more messages. No more contact. I had a feeling Nelis wouldn't listen.

'You can sort it out yourselves from now on. Nothing to do with me.'

'You go back and tell Armour, if he wants a deal we have to meet.'

I was the go-between, Armour had said. Passing messages. I should have known better. It wouldn't just be one message! I backed down the steps, not turning from Nelis. Not taking my eyes from him. I was almost away when he said it.

'So . . . you're Armour's boy, are you?'

19

Armour's boy, he had called me. Was that the way he saw me. Armour's boy?

I wasn't Armour's boy. I stormed away from him, and knew without even really thinking about it that I wasn't going home. Not then. I was going to Armour's house. I would pass on the message and let Armour know I was not his boy. Not now. Not ever.

I knew where he lived. Me and Sean had passed his house one day when we were up visiting Sean's auntie. She lived in the Drumshantie estate. Or the 'Drummie' as we call it here. Armour's turf. Sean had pointed the house out to me. A bungalow on a corner. Stone lions guarding the front gates. 'To show he's the king around here, I suppose,' Sean had said.

And Armour's words came back to me. *Leo – lion – the symbol of kings.*

At the town centre I jumped on the bus that would take me up to the Drummie. I hardly noticed anything, I had so much going on in my head. Couldn't even be sure why I was going there.

But of course I did know why. Because I wanted it over. I'd pass on the message and it would be finished. And I would get on with my life. Forget all about Armour.

As I approached his house the stone lions seemed to be watching me. Wondering why I was there too. I glanced around. What if someone saw me? Someone who knew my mum or dad? What if Sean heard I was here?

In that second I would have turned on my heels and left. But it was at that moment the front door was hauled open and Armour stood there. He was wearing a designer T-shirt, as blue as his eyes. He was smiling broadly.

'Leo, hello, what brings you up here?'

I blurted the words out. 'You never told me Nelis would give me a message to give to you. He gave me a message. That's why I came here.'

'And you brought his message right here. Thanks.'

'I'm only going to tell you this and that's me finished. Right?'

'Right, Leo. Right,' he said.

I didn't move closer. I was ready to run as soon as I told him. Armour seemed to understand. 'What was his message, Leo?'

'He says he wants to meet you face to face. That's the only way he'll make a deal.' I drew in my breath. 'And don't ask me to go back to him. I won't do it.'

'Wouldn't ask you to,' he said at once. 'I'll handle it from now on. You've done enough.'

I turned to go.

'Do you want a lift?'

I didn't look back. 'No. I'm fine.'

'Have you got enough money for the bus?'

'I'm fine,' I said again.

He wasn't going to let me go. I was sure of it.

'Thank you,' he said. 'Thank you, Leo.'

Hardly the words of a killer. A murderer, a gang boss. Armour said 'thank you' and closed the door. He even offered me a lift. He asked if I had enough money for the bus. He was trying to make peace with Nelis.

McCrae had been evil. The town was better off without him.

The town was better off – thanks to Armour.

My dad had a job – thanks to Armour.

I was mixed up and just to mix me up even more, the

104

Bissett Boys were hanging around the bus stop at the town centre. As soon as I stepped on to the pavement they clocked me.

They turned and stared at me. And I stared right back. Wasn't afraid to do that, not now. I didn't turn and run. It was the Bissett Boys who bolted. They saw me and they were off, running in the opposite direction.

They knew.

I was Armour's boy. Had they heard that too? Nelis's words came back to me.

I was safe from the Bissett Boys – thanks to Armour.

No, I wouldn't see him again. I would have nothing to do with him.

But the thought wouldn't go away – Armour wasn't so bad.

20

A week went by. Nothing more from Armour. It was all over. I was sure of it. And Aidan's birthday party was coming up. I met Sean in town on the Saturday so we could get him a present between us.

'What were you doing up the Drummie last Thursday? My big cousin saw you on the bus.'

The first thing he asked me. The last thing I wanted to hear. I should have known someone would have seen me, but did it have to be Sean's cousin? Sean had cousins everywhere. Family spread all over the town. Of course one of them had seen me. I had to think fast. But not fast enough for Sean.

'Who do you know up there?'

I still didn't have an answer. Now he was looking at me suspiciously. 'What's the problem?'

'I'm trying to think,' I said. 'I mean . . . remember. I

mean – last Thursday – how am I supposed to remember that? Who do you think I am, Brain of Britain?'

'I'm only asking.'

'I was going a message for my mum.' A lie, blurted out without thinking it through. Always a mistake.

'Your mum asked you to go a message up the Drummie for her?'

Stupid, stupid thing to say. The Drummie was one of the worst areas in the town. My mum and dad, like Sean's, picked us up everywhere we went. She would be hardly likely to send me up there by myself.

'I know, that's what I thought. Don't know what she was thinking about.'

Still he wouldn't let it go. 'What kind of message?'

This time I snapped at him. 'It was private, right? None of your business.'

His jaw dropped. He looked hurt. No wonder. I'd never talked to my best mate like that before.

'Secrets,' he said. And for a second I thought he knew. He knew everything. 'You're keeping secrets – and we always said we'd tell each other everything.'

I had a quick answer for that. 'I can't tell you my mum's secrets though, can I?'

He still looked hurt. At that moment there was a

distance between us wider than a chasm. And I told myself, from now on no more secrets. I'd never keep anything from him again.

But it was soon put behind us. We never stayed mad at each other for long. And anyway, we had too much fun picking a present for Aidan. We decided on buying a PlayStation game between us, preferably one we could borrow from him and forget to return.

'There's a new vampire one out,' I reminded Sean.

'Aidan hates vampires,' Sean said.

That decided us. Vampires it was. Then he'd probably not even ask for it back.

We were just paying for it when we heard the commotion behind us – people muttering, calling across to each other. Something was happening.

An old lady passed us by. 'It's like the blinking Wild West in this blinking town.'

'What's she talking about?' I said to Sean.

We didn't have to wait too long for our answer.

'There's an armed siege going on up the Baird Road shops. SWAT teams up there and everything. Place is cordoned off.'

I looked at Sean. He looked at me.

'An armed siege?' Sean couldn't keep the excitement

out of his voice. 'This is too good to miss. Come on.' He began to drag me out of the shop. 'We'll get the bus.'

I didn't want to go. Something told me not to go. But how could I explain that to Sean? So I let myself be dragged along after him.

The bus was diverted because of the siege but Sean and I got off and made our way to the shops, pushing in as close as we could.

We weren't the only ones drawn to the scene. The streets were crowded. Everyone was standing behind a long line of yellow tape. It was hard to get a good view, but somehow, Sean and me managed it. 'It's funny to see the cops with guns, isn't it?' Sean said.

Not only guns but protective vests and helmets.

'I know.'

If we lived in America we would be used to it, but here in our town it looked wrong somehow.

'He's got a hostage inside the shops. And he's got a gun,' somebody called out.

Sean gaped at me. 'A hostage situation?' he said. 'This is getting better by the second.'

Only weeks ago I would have been as excited as he was. Now I felt a cold chill go through me. 'Who's in there?' I asked.

'He let the other people go – a woman and her wee boy,' I heard someone say.

Another shout went up. 'He's still got the shop manager in there. At gunpoint.'

'Hope he's getting paid overtime,' someone else said. Typical, even in the middle of something awful someone in our town saw the funny side.

'What happened anyway?' I asked no one in particular.

'Murder,' someone answered. 'They were trying to arrest him for murder and he ran.'

'Who did he murder?' Sean asked.

That cold chill froze my bones. I had a feeling I knew the answer.

'McCrae,' someone said.

My legs wobbled. Armour was in there. They'd found him – at last he was being arrested. Would he think now I'd told on him? Was he even now peering through the venetian blinds in the shop, could see me standing here, convinced it must be me who had brought all this on him?

If I'd had the courage I would have dragged Sean away from there right then.

The police, using a megaphone, were urging him to

release his hostage, to give himself up.

'Wish I'd brought my camera,' Sean said. He turned to me. 'You got your phone? Take a video of this.'

He wanted a video of the police rushing the building, bringing Armour out, his arms pinioned behind his back. I could see it all in my imagination, like a movie. See the scene zoom in on his blue eyes as they focused on me.

'We could be here for ages, Sean. Come on we'll just go home.'

Sean looked at me as if I was mad. 'You've got to be joking. Miss this?' He nudged the man in front of us again. 'So who did it?'

It was me who almost answered him. *Armour did it.* I almost said it. Almost spoke his name.

But the man in front got there first. 'You know that guy, Sheridan? McCrae shot his daughter? Turns out it was him that killed McCrae all the time.'

21

It wasn't Armour in there at all. It was Andy Sheridan. He'd been back in the papers several times since McCrae had been killed.

I HOPE HE ROTS IN HELL

I could still see the headline. McCrae had shot his daughter. Ruined his life, he'd said. He was glad he was dead.

But Sheridan hadn't killed him. I knew that.

He was in those shops with a gun and a hostage and everyone seemed to be satisfied that he must be McCrae's killer.

But I knew he wasn't.

'This is dead exciting,' Sean said. 'I wonder how long he'll be in there. Hey, maybe we'll be here all night.'

But we weren't there all night. Half an hour later the shop manager stumbled through the glass-fronted doors. His hands were held high, he was calling out in a frightened voice, 'Don't shoot!'

'He's giving himself up,' someone in the crowd shouted out.

The man was white with shock, and an officer ran forward and threw a blanket over his shoulders and hurried him behind the line of policemen.

The crowd grew deathly silent, waiting. A moment later there was a communal gasp as a rifle came flying out of the doorway. It clattered on the ground.

'Is that what a sawn-off shotgun looks like?' Sean nudged me.

It took me back to the night I had found Nelis's stash of guns. Is that where Sheridan had got this one? Bought from Nelis?

'Look how they're lifting it. Don't want to contaminate the evidence.' Sean sounded as if he was having great fun. 'That could be the murder weapon.'

A policeman was slipping it into a long plastic bag, careful not to touch it, not to wipe it off any fingerprints or DNA.

'Aye,' Sean went on, 'they'll be able to tell if that's the

murder weapon all right. If the bullets match, if there's any DNA on it. You name it. The evidence never lies,' Sean said, as if he was an expert. 'Even after all this time . . . they'll know.'

But that wasn't the murder weapon, I knew that. I knew exactly where the murder weapon was, that is if Armour hadn't come back and retrieved it. And I doubted he would have done that. There was still a big police presence in that area. Wouldn't be worth the risk.

There was a commotion at the doorway. The police raised their rifles.

'He's coming out,' someone shouted.

And Andy Sheridan appeared. Emerging into the sunlight, even more white-faced than his hostage. He had his hands locked on top of his head and immediately he came out the police swooped around him, pulling his hands down, handcuffing him.

But they weren't rough with him. I could see that. We all could. It was as if they wished they didn't have to do this at all.

They didn't want him to be guilty.

He's not *guilty!* I wanted to shout that out to them. *I know who's guilty!*

Why didn't I? I was still afraid. Afraid to speak out, to

unzip my lip. But could there be something else that stopped me?

Some kind of warped loyalty.

Armour had got my dad a job. He'd got the Bissett Boys off my back. I was grateful for that.

The crowd stayed silent as Mr Sheridan was led to a police car. Then all of a sudden a cheer went up. A cheer of support, and that made him turn to the crowd.

He looked tired and vulnerable. I felt so sorry for him.

'I'm being framed!' he shouted.

The cheers grew louder. Sheridan was pushed gently into the police car. He even managed a sad smile at us. The car moved away, and then the crowd broke, muttering their support for Sheridan.

'He should get a medal for shooting that guy, not jail.'

In spite of him shouting his innocence, they were willing to believe he might be the killer. But they understood why he'd done it. They supported him. They just didn't think he was innocent.

'Who could blame the man?' I heard someone else say.

Sean was reluctant to go. 'We should hang about

here. Maybe we could find some clues they've missed.'

It was exactly what we would have done just a few weeks ago. But now I hardly listened to him. I wanted away from here – but not to go home. I couldn't go home. Not yet. There was somewhere else I had to go.

'Are you feeling all right?' Sean asked.

I had hardly said a word. Couldn't share in his excitement. No wonder he thought I was ill.

'I seem to be asking you that a lot at the moment.' He looked at me thoughtfully. 'You're acting funny. Is anything wrong?'

'I just don't feel that good,' was all I said. Not enough of an explanation.

We hardly spoke as I walked him to his bus. He knew there was something I wasn't telling him, and it hurt. I waved him off on the bus, but Sean didn't wave back. I waited till his bus had turned the corner out of sight before I began walking. But I didn't head for home. I was heading for a place I swore I would never go again.

Armour's house.

The stone lions still stared at me as I walked up the drive. The silver Mercedes sat there. It was as if Armour had been waiting for me, watching for me, expecting me.

The door was hauled open. And he was standing there. His shirtsleeves were rolled up almost to his shoulder, revealing his tanned, bulging biceps. The neck of his shirt lay open. He looked as if he had just stood up from the table, finishing his meal. He smiled, a big wide smile.

'I've been expecting you.' He stepped back. 'Come on in.'

I only hesitated for a second. Behind him down the hall I could see a woman in the kitchen. His wife. Her black hair was piled high on her head. She wore too much make-up. She had a nail salon in the town.

Everyone said it was a front for something much more sinister. She turned and flashed a smile at me and lifted a giggling little girl on to her hip. Then she closed the door of the kitchen. We were alone in the hall.

'How did you know I was coming?' I asked, as Armour led me into his front room.

'It's all round the town. Sheridan's been arrested.' The room was all dark leather furniture and bookcases. 'If you hadn't come I would have searched you out. I have some explaining to do, don't I?'

He motioned me to one of the leather chairs. I seemed to sink deep into it. Then he sat across from me.

'Explain what? What is there to explain?' I wanted him to tell me. And he did.

'You think I'm going to let an innocent man take the blame for something I did?' He wasn't expecting me to answer him. He went on. 'Sheridan probably won't even be charged. There's no real evidence against him. He's his own worst enemy. Ranting on constantly about wanting McCrae dead. Did you see that headline in the paper?'

I nodded.

'Then he goes and takes a hostage? The cops had to

arrest him. They had no choice. But the charges won't stick.'

He smiled again. There was something about his smile that reassured me. 'I won't let them, Leo. But they'll have to keep him in jail for a while anyway. I mean, he did have a gun. He did take a man hostage. They'll have to charge him with that.'

That made me feel a bit better. He was right. Mr Sheridan wasn't completely innocent.

'And he's probably safer in jail anyway. McCrae's men would be after him if he wasn't.' And that sounded sensible too. 'I can't do anything about it now, Leo. I hope you understand that. Not till I make this deal with Nelis. Then the fighting will be over.'

Did he mean he was going to give himself up? He seemed to be able to read my mind.

'No. I have no intention of confessing. But Andy Sheridan's gone through so much already, losing his daughter like that. I'll make sure he has an alibi. I'll make sure no charges will stick.'

'You promise?'

'You have my word.'

It was the best I was going to get. I stood up. The living-room door swung open and the little girl ran in.

Armour swooped her up into his arms. She giggled and he kissed her cheek. He looked just like any other loving dad. Like my dad.

'Thanks for coming, Leo,' he said. 'Any other boy would have run to the police. I knew you would come here – let me explain. You're one boy I can really trust.' He hesitated as if he wanted to say more. 'I'll find a way to thank you.'

'You've thanked me enough,' I said quickly.

'I could so use a boy like you. Someone I can trust – especially with this business with Nelis. Even he trusts you.' He hesitated again. I knew something else was coming. 'I don't want to ask you this. I shouldn't be asking you this . . . but this business is so important to me. I can't involve any of my people. I don't want them to know what I'm planning till it's done. See, if they knew I wanted peace, Leo . . . it would make me look weak in their eyes. So there's none of them I can trust with this.'

The little girl tightened her arms round his neck, snuggled into him. Maybe if she hadn't done that right at that moment I would have walked away. But a man couldn't be all bad if his little girl loved him so much . . . could he? And I knew what was coming. Knew what he was going to say.

'If I need to pass another message on to Nelis, can I count on you? I don't know if he would trust anyone else now.'

I wanted to say no. I wanted to run.

And I didn't.

The only one he'll trust. The only one Armour could rely on.

Armour was only trying to make peace. He wasn't so bad.

I heard myself telling him, 'Yes.'

As I walked away from the house, past those stone lions, a voice seemed to be whispering to me. A voice I should have listened to.

'Now you really are Armour's boy.'

23

Dad was on his high horse again when I arrived back home. He hardly noticed I was so late. Too much else on his mind. An armed siege. Sheridan arrested.

He was storming about the living room. 'Where are we living? Is this Chicago in the 1920s? I want my children to be safe. I want them to be able to walk the streets in safety!' He stopped. 'I want guns off the streets.'

He had clearly been going on about it for ages. I saw my mum rolling her eyes at me in a 'nothing can shut him up' kind of way.

'Dave,' she said. 'You talk as if you're giving a speech. I agree with you, but do something about it if it means that much to you.'

He sat down. 'I think I might.'

Wee David turned from his Nintendo game and looked at me. 'Is Dad angry at me, Leo?'

My dad smiled then. 'Angry at you, son? How could I ever be angry at you?'

David flashed him a big smile. It would be hard, impossible, not to smile back at our David.

But Dad was angry. Angry about the guns, angry about everything that was going on in the town. He was on the phone later to Sean's dad and all their talk was about what had happened at the shops that day. And when Sean phoned me later on my mobile it seemed his dad was just as angry as mine.

'What are they like?' Sean said. 'He's going on about Andy Sheridan being driven to it – a man like that wouldn't know about how to get a gun. You get guns too easily here, my dad says. Anyway, he doesn't think Sheridan did it. I don't think anybody does. Not really.' He waited. Waited for me to agree with him. 'You don't think he did it, do you?'

It was so hard not to tell him then that I knew everything. But all I said was, 'No, I don't think he did it.'

'I was dying to tell my dad he shouted, "I'm being framed!" when they were putting him in the car, but he would have went spare if he knew I'd gone up there. Did you tell your dad?'

'No,' I said. 'I didn't tell him.'

But I knew my voice didn't have the excitement that Sean's had.

'Are you OK, Leo? You sound funny.'

'I'm fine,' I said at once. 'Fine.'

Sean was waiting for me at the school gates next morning. I smiled at him, but Sean didn't smile back. His face was grim.

'What's wrong with you?' I asked.

'You never told me you were going back up the Drummie last night.'

That blinking cousin of his again must have spotted me. And my first awful thought – did he see me going into Armour's house? Did anyone?

I didn't know what to say to Sean. 'Sorry' didn't seem to be enough.

'Has your mum got a boyfriend up there?'

That shook me. I had told him my mum had sent me up there the first time. He was going to think my mum was cheating on my dad unless I told him the truth . . . or came up with a believable lie.

Because I couldn't tell him the truth. But another lie wouldn't form in my brain.

'Of course, she hasn't,' I said. 'My mum? You're

joking.' But my voice was weak.

'You left me at the bus stop yesterday and went right up the Drummie without telling me. What for?'

I couldn't tell him. I only shrugged. The best form of defence is attack. The thought came to me. 'Come on, Sean, we're not Siamese twins – I don't have to tell you everything, do I?'

There was anger in Sean's face. It went red with it. 'Right. I'll remember that, *pal*!'

He spat the last word out sarcastically then he swung away from me and stalked off.

You think that was the end of a beautiful friendship?

No, it wasn't.

Not then.

24

Saturday was Aidan's party. By that time our argument was forgotten. Me and Sean met in town and made our way together to the hall Aidan's mum had booked for the party.

'I don't know why he asked girls,' I said, watching giggling girls from our class going into the hall in front of us.

'You know why,' Sean said. 'Because he fancies Veronika.'

'You say that all the time.'

'You watch him, pal. This is his chance to get right in there.'

'Veronika might not come,' I said.

But even as I said it, I saw her. I'd never seen her out of school uniform before and she looked different. Better – a green top, jeans. She always wore her hair pulled back at school, but today it fell about her shoulders and when she turned her head it seemed to move with her like silk.

'Put your eyes back in their sockets, pal.' Sean laughed. 'Today's your chance. Chat her up.'

'I'm not going to chat her up.' Because what if she snubbed me? Or what if she preferred big Aidan?

Rubbish! The sensible part of my brain told me.

But even by the time Sean and I had walked into the hall, big Aidan had moved right in. Standing beside her, chatting away. I didn't stand a chance with her.

At least, I thought, looking at the buffet table – comforting myself – there's plenty to eat.

We could hardly hear ourselves, the music was so loud, so me and Sean made a beeline for the table groaning with food, and we got stuck in.

'Wow! You could feed a small African country with what's on this table alone,' Sean said.

I stuck two cocktail sausages in my mouth as if they were fangs and tapped him on the shoulder.

'I need your blood,' I moaned in my best Transylvanian accent. But it's hard to talk with two cocktail sausages trapped in your teeth.

And it was exactly then that Veronika appeared at my side.

'Excuse me,' she said, leaning over me for a paper plate. I turned quickly and she took one look at my sausage fangs and began to giggle.

I swallowed both of them and started to choke. Her and Sean patted me on the back at the same time.

'Are you OK, Leo?'

I tried to answer her but it's hard to talk when you're choking to death.

'I think he might need the kiss of life, Veronika,' Sean said and I poked him in the ribs.

'Or the Heimlich manoeuvre. Are you any good at that, Veronika?'

Veronika looked puzzled. Her English was good, but maybe not that good. 'Heimlich who? Did he write something?'

That only made me laugh, and to my embarrassment the sausage that had stuck in my throat shot out of my mouth and flew across the room.

Aidan came running up. 'Come on, Leo. You're coughing all over my birthday buffet.'

That only made me laugh and choke all the more.

Sean started to laugh too, and to my surprise, so did Veronika.

It was only when Aidan saw her laughing that he began to see the funny side.

'Hey, I could be dying here!' I choked out. Laughing and choking at the same time. My eyes were running and Veronika was still patting my back.

'Want to have a dance, Veronika?' Aidan asked her.

The moment was going to be over. She was going off with Aidan. But her green eyes turned from Aidan back to me.

Sean nudged me. In fact he almost pushed me against her.

'I was going to ask the same thing,' was what I tried to say, but I couldn't get the words out.

To my complete astonishment Veronika turned back to Aidan and said, 'I think Leo asked me first.'

And I hadn't. I had been too busy choking to death.

Why had she said that? Could it be because she really wanted to dance with me?

Dance?

Me?

It was Sean who pushed me on to the floor. I kind of stood there, trying to move in time to the music. I saw

Shannon watch me with her mouth open. As if she'd never seen anything like it in her life before.

But I hardly noticed Shannon. Didn't have time to get annoyed at her. I was dancing with Veronika. She was good. She had natural rhythm. She looked at me and smiled and mouthed something at me. Couldn't make out a word she was saying. The music was still too loud. But suddenly, it didn't matter. I saw Sean at the side of the dance floor, watching me with a big smile on his face, giving me the thumbs up. Veronika was smiling too – a kind of shy smile. She had picked me over Aidan. Even though I danced like a demented rabbit.

I began to enjoy myself.

This was going to be a great party.

25

That Saturday night just got better. Veronika didn't leave my side. We danced. Well, she danced – I jiggled about. We went back to the buffet table together and this time I didn't choke. We danced again. We sat at the side and talked. She told me about her dad and her mum – and her little sister, who sounded just as daft as my wee brother. We laughed together.

I had this strange feeling that there were going to be lots of other days for me to find out more about Veronika and her family. Glancing around I could see other people thought that too. Aidan couldn't stop glaring daggers at me. Shannon was watching too. As if she was amazed and annoyed at the same time.

Her mate fancied me. ME! Who knew?

And Sean all the time walking about with a big grin on his face as if it was all down to him.

I was just as amazed. Amazed that Veronika seemed to prefer me to big Aidan.

'So your dad's a dentist,' I said. I think it was about the fourth time I'd asked her the same thing.

'Yes, and I am so happy because now he can stay here. In this country. Now he has a permanent work permit.

'Oh, that's good,' I said. 'Maybe I could make an appointment with him – to get a check-up.'

I could hardly believe I'd said that. Suggesting I go to the dentist. What was happening to me!

'I'll see what I can do,' Veronika said. 'But I've heard them say he's more of a butcher than a dentist.'

The shock must have shown on my face and she started to laugh. 'It's a joke. Shannon said it first and it was so funny. You don't think it's funny?'

'It's not that.' I glanced across at the miserable Shannon. 'I'm just amazed that Shannon's got a sense of humour.' I looked back at Veronika. 'How did you and Shannon ever become friends?'

'My first day at school. You probably don't remember.' She blushed, but I did remember. Remember how she'd blushed the same way, standing in front of the class as Mrs McIndoo introduced her.

'Shannon spoke to me right away. I thought she was

going to pick a fight, she looks so scary. But she was so nice. Made me feel at home. She's my best friend now.'

Veronika turned her dazzling smile on Shannon. Even then Shannon didn't smile back. But to my horror she started swaggering towards us.

'Are you having a good time, Shannon?' Veronika called out to her.

'How can I be having a good time when you've bagged the best-looking boy at the party?' Then she stuck her two fingers down her throat as if she was making herself sick. '– I don't think.'

Veronika giggled. Moved a little closer to me. That was all. As if she really *did* believe I was the best looking boy at the party and she really *had* bagged me.

'Want to go to the lavvy?' Shannon asked.

'You must be doing wonders for Veronika's English,' I said.

'Ladies. Toilets. Is that better?' She grabbed Veronika. 'It's still the lavvy.'

Veronika turned to me. 'Will you wait for me here, Leo?'

Now it was my turn to blush. 'Aye. Nae bother.' All I could think of to say.

Even at the door of the girls' toilets she turned and

smiled at me as if she was assuring herself I was still there.

In my wildest dreams I couldn't have believed the night would go so well. Veronika had come on to me. Veronika. Who would have thought she liked me?

I was so lost in my own thoughts I didn't notice Frankie Mitchell come up beside me at the buffet table.

'Well, this is a surprise,' he said.

'What?'

'Who'd have thought Veronika fancied you?'

I was about to say I had been thinking the same thing myself, till I realised he was trying to insult me. 'Stranger things have happened,' I said.

'Came right out of the blue, that did,' he said.

'Don't know about that.' I looked at him and wished I had the courage to stuff a jelly doughnut in his face.

'One minute everybody thinks it's big Aidan she's after, and the next – she's stuck to you like glue. What did you do, Leo? Put a spell on her? Blackmail her?' He started to laugh. 'Maybe you sold your soul to the devil, eh?'

He thought it was funny. He was laughing as he moved away. And I felt as if an icy chill filled the room.

Blackmail. Maybe you sold your soul to the devil.

I had never noticed Veronika even look my way, hardly a glance. And now tonight, she had come to me. No wonder everyone looked so surprised.

I didn't want to think what I was thinking.

'I'll find a way to thank you,' Armour had said.

Was this his way of thanking me?

But he couldn't do that, could he?

Only a few days ago, Veronika's dad was afraid he was going to lose his work permit. Be sent back to Poland. Veronika was happy now. They were going to stay. Had Armour helped that along? Had he then threatened that he could have the whole family shipped back to Poland unless she pretended to like me?

No! I was just being silly. Armour didn't even know I liked Veronika.

But he'd known about the Bissett Boys.

He'd known my dad needed a job. Armour knew everything.

Now I understood.

Big Aidan being so amazed that Veronika had chosen me. Shannon's look of puzzlement. She was Veronika's best friend and even she couldn't believe Veronika preferred me. It had come as a surprise to her too.

The music was too loud. I could see Sean on the floor

dancing almost as badly as me. In those moments, everything fell into place.

And I was angry. I wanted to go home. Didn't want to stay there a minute longer. Nothing was real.

Veronika came out of the toilets and started walking towards me. That false smile on her face.

He can't see you in here, I wanted to shout at her. *You don't have to smile at me in here.*

She lifted two cups of cherry cola and came up to me. My eyes hadn't left her. Had she noticed that I wasn't smiling?

She handed me the cups. 'Here, I got you a drink.'

I wanted to yell and shout and scream. I was angry at the world. But most of all I was angry with Veronika.

I pushed the cola back at her. Too hard. The cups flew into the air, the cherry cola splattered out and fell like drops of blood all over her face, through her blonde hair, soaked into her green top.

'I don't want anything from you,' I yelled at her. 'Away you go, back to Poland.'

26

I stormed out of the hall, pushing people aside as I did. I don't know what I was thinking. I remember the music screeching off, but I can't be sure. I was too angry. Too mixed up.

My collar was grabbed and I was hauled back before I'd even reached the door. I swung round, my fist closed and ready for a fight. It was Sean. His face was red with a fury I'd never seen in him before.

'What did you do that for? What's your problem?' he shouted.

Behind him, still at the table, almost in shadow, I could see Veronika. She was crying, surrounded by girls trying to dry her off, comforting her.

I pushed Sean away. 'You don't know anything.' How could I explain? There was too much to explain now.

Sean lunged at me. He took me by surprise, brought

me down. 'Something's changed you!' I heard him say.

I didn't answer. Didn't say a word. I landed a punch against his face. It was as if at that moment all the fear and anger and confusion I'd been feeling over the past weeks exploded out of me. That was it. I'd never fought so hard, punched anyone with such venom as I punched my best mate. We rolled around the floor kicking at each other, entangled in each other. We were encircled by everyone at the party. Cheering and shouting. But not cheering me. They were all against me.

'Get right into him, Sean.'

'Give him a good punch for me.'

Their antagonism only made me angrier. I felt the whole world was against me and I hadn't done anything wrong. I began punching like a wild man. At one point I punched him so hard blood spurted from his mouth. Splashed on me.

I'd never seen Sean so angry. He bared his blood-stained teeth at me and punched me right back. I managed to turn my face away at the last minute. His fist thumped against my ear. I saw the room spin.

It was Aidan's mum who stopped it. Pushing through the crowd, yelling and shouting her rage. She hauled us both to our feet.

'What do you think you're playing at? This is Aidan's birthday party.'

I didn't wait around to answer. Didn't wait around to hear them all blaming me. I yanked myself away from her and stumbled out into the street. And then I ran all the way home.

My dad knew all about it by the time I arrived back at the house. Aidan's mum had phoned him. And he blamed me too. But even then he had got the whole wrong end of the stick. It would have been funny any other time. He thought – how many of them were thinking the same thing? That me and Sean had been fighting over Veronika. Over a girl!

Yet what could I tell him when he asked? The truth? *No* chance. He kept asking over and over again for me to explain what happened. And I had no answer.

'Sean's your best friend. Apologise to him. Apologise to this girl.'

But I couldn't. And I would not.

He sent me to bed early. As I lay there the door creaked open and David crawled in along the floor, like a miniature commando.

'Want to play soldiers?' he whispered. As if the enemy was already nearby, could hear his every word.

'No, David. Not tonight.'

He came closer, sat on the bed beside me. 'Have you been a bad boy, Leo?'

And it was unfair because I hadn't been a bad boy – had I? What had I done that was so wrong? I was trying to protect my family. My friend. Yet I was the one being made to feel as if I was guilty of something.

It wasn't fair.

The only one who made me feel special . . . was Armour. I couldn't help thinking it. He trusted me. He believed me. He knew I was trying to do the right thing.

I think that night changed everything.

I felt I had burned my boats.

There was no going back now.

27

Sean didn't phone me the next day. And I didn't phone him. I lay in bed most of the day, till early evening when my dad came up to my room and insisted I go to six o'clock Mass with him. I wanted to say no, but I knew he half hoped that Sean might be there too and we would have a chance to make up.

'I mean, you're not going to break up a friendship over a girl,' he said as we walked to church.

Still thinking we'd been fighting over Veronika. I tried not to, but all through Mass my eyes kept scanning the church looking for Sean. But he wasn't there. And I told myself it didn't matter.

Because we hadn't been fighting over Veronika – not really. It went a lot deeper than that. I had been keeping secrets, and Sean knew it.

Dad put his hand on my shoulder as we walked home.

He bought me an ice cream at the Orangefield Café. Trying to console me.

'He'll be at school tomorrow. It'll be fine. You'll see. Bet he'll phone you later.'

But it wasn't Sean who phoned me as I sat in my room that night, watching *C.S.I.*

It was Armour.

'Can you talk?' he asked.

David was in bed. Mum and Dad were downstairs watching their favourite programmes. Yes, I could talk. But did I want to?

'What do you want?'

'I heard about the fight,' he said.

Heard about a fight at a boy's birthday party? Why was that so important? And how did he find out about it?

He answered my unasked question: 'I'm keeping my eye on you, Leo.'

I wanted to shout at him, *It was all your fault.* But all I said was, 'I don't need your thanks. I told you that.'

There was quiet on the line. I was afraid my dad would come in and catch me talking to him any second.

'What do you mean, Leo? My thanks?'

'Telling Veronika to be nice to me. That's what I mean,' I said.

There was another long pause. 'Veronika? Who's Veronika?'

Now it was my turn to be quiet. Stunned into silence. He didn't know about Veronika. Didn't know anything about her. It hadn't been him. Nothing to do with him at all. He hadn't threatened her family. He hadn't helped her dad to stay in this country. He didn't know what I was talking about.

I saw it all again in my mind's eye. Veronika's puzzled eyes when I shouted at her. She hadn't known what I was talking about either. I had blown it all for nothing.

I should have known Armour wouldn't have gone that far. I felt stupid, felt like screaming.

'Is she your girlfriend?' he asked.

'No!' I snapped the word out. I was sorry now I'd even mentioned her name.

What had I done?

'I just wanted to make sure you were all right.'

'Thanks,' I said.

'Bet you can handle yourself anyway. Don't ever have to worry about you in a fight.'

'I was fighting with my best mate.' That was what hurt more than anything – I had been fighting with Sean.

'In my business you can't have mates, Leo. You have

to keep your friends at arm's length.' He said it as if it was as important to me as it was to him.

I closed the phone just as my mum opened the bedroom door. She glanced at the phone. 'Was that Sean?'

I shook my head. 'No. I was just checking in case he'd texted me.'

'*C.S.I.*'s almost finished. So time to put your light out,' she said.

I lay awake for ages, thinking. I'd had a fight with my best mate for nothing. It could have been a wonderful party. I could be lying here looking forward to tomorrow. To being with Sean, maybe being with Veronika. And I'd blown it. All for nothing.

And I couldn't even explain to them why I'd done it. No apology to Sean or Veronika would be enough without that explanation.

And then just as I was drifting off into an uneasy sleep, another alarming thought came to me.

How did Armour get my mobile number?

28

Next day only made things worse. I had planned to apologise. To give it a try, even if it meant telling a lie. First thing I had to do was apologise to Veronika. I went over and over it in my mind, finding exactly the right words. And in my imaginary conversation she kept asking why, and I didn't have the answer. And I couldn't think up a good enough lie.

And what would I say to Sean? What *could* I say to him? It had been a mistake. Veronika's dad wasn't being blackmailed by Armour. I'd been wrong.

So, in the end, I decided I would say nothing. Just maybe, day by day, try to make things better.

I knew as soon as I walked through the school gates even that wouldn't happen.

Sean stood at the big entrance door with Aidan by his side. Veronika was there too. Flanked by them both. Under protection. That's what it looked like. As if they thought I would run at her. Bring her down in a commando-style attack.

She kept her eyes down, staring at the ground. But she knew I was there. They all knew I was there. Sean stared at me boldly. His eyes didn't leave me as I walked closer. I glanced round the playground and they were all watching me. As if they knew something I didn't. When I looked at them they would all look away quickly, as if they didn't want me to see them watching me.

Only Sean's eyes never left me.

Then Sean broke away from Aidan and Veronika and strode towards me. Now was my chance to say something, to apologise for a moment of madness. He was my mate. Had been my mate since Primary 1. Surely he would understand?

He was feet from me and he shouted out his words. 'Think you're a big man now, eh? Think we're gonnae be scared of you!'

What was he talking about?

He made a rush at me, grabbed my shirt, yanked me towards him. 'Well, I'm not scared of you. I just can't understand you. Can't believe you would have anything to do with Armour.'

I plucked his hands from me. Things were beginning to fall into place. His nosy cousin again. He must have seen me going into Armour's house.

'None of your business if I go and see Armour.'

I knew as soon as the words were out of my mouth that I had got it wrong.

'You went to Armour's *house*? Are you mad?' He was shocked, astonished. 'You actually went up to Armour's house?'

I looked around them all, still watching me. But what did they know?

Sean gave me the answer. 'Seems the Bissett Boys spread the word. You're Armour's boy. I didn't believe it. I told everybody that was crazy talk. But . . . it's true, isn't it?'

I was trying desperately to think of a way to explain it all.

'Was that what made you bold enough to throw cola all over Veronika? Big man,' he sneered. 'I thought you would tell me it wasn't true. The Bissett Boys were lying. And you tell me you go to Armour's house? That's what you were doing up the Drummie, wasn't it?'

'Maybe Armour's not so bad.'

Sean stepped back from me as if I had hit him with a

brick. 'Armour's not so bad? Are you listening to yourself. It's all true, isn't it? You are Armour's boy. That's what the Bissett Boys called you.' He spat on the ground as if I disgusted him.

I wanted to tell him. Armour wanted peace. I was helping him. Armour wasn't as bad as everybody made out.

'He's evil. You know that. He's got a hand in everything that's bad in this town.'

'You're just repeating what your dad says.'

'Your dad says it too.'

I swallowed. 'Maybe my dad's wrong.'

'And Armour's right? I can't believe you just said that.'

Why couldn't he trust me? I wanted to explain, but there was nothing I could say. And anyway, Sean didn't want an answer. Didn't need one. He took another step away from me.

'You keep back from me from now on, Leo. You're no mate of mine. You'll never be my mate again.'

You'll never be my mate again. The words whispered themselves in my head all day.

I stood alone in the yard at break time. Sat alone in

the canteen during lunch. The only one who looked at me was Shannon and that was only to sneer. I'd never felt so lonely in my life.

I walked home from school that day, alone. And when my mobile rang I felt it was the first time someone had wanted to talk to me all day.

'Hello, Leo.' The now familiar voice. Armour. 'You said I could rely on you. Is that still the case?' As if I could refuse. 'It's to do with Nelis. You're the only one he'll talk to.'

At least someone trusted me. Knew I was trying to do the right thing.

And why shouldn't I do it?

I had no one else now.

I was Armour's boy.

29

My dad was on a crusade. Having a job gave him back the confidence he'd lost.

The confidence to take charge, to get things done.

He was going to do something to clean up this town, he said.

A few nights later when he picked me up from football practice he told me he'd been to the police station. Talking over what could be done.

This was a football practice I hadn't actually attended. Mum had dropped me off and I had hoofed it to the place I had arranged to meet Armour. He wanted me to meet up with Nelis again. Armour was trying to work out a diplomatic solution, he told me, the way you do with terrorists or hostage takers. He wanted to come to some kind of a deal with Nelis. He wanted the trouble in the town to stop.

Same as my dad.

So what was I doing wrong in helping him?

He had me back at the school grounds well before my dad came to pick me up.

'Sean not there tonight?' Dad asked as soon as I got in the car. He asked me the same thing every day. Had I spoken to Sean? Had Sean spoken to me? Hoping that the rift was healed. That Sean and I had talked, had made up. Then he'd shake his head and say, 'You'll be friends again before long.'

He'd even been on the phone to Sean's dad – and that night I had held my breath waiting for him to burst back into the room demanding to know why I was seeing Armour.

But he didn't. Sean hadn't told his dad.

Sean was no grass.

'I've been at that police station since I finished work,' Dad told me.

'They've found you out at last then? You're the serial killer the whole country's been looking for.'

He grinned. 'We talked about having a gun amnesty. So anyone who owns a gun can hand it in, no charges, no questions asked. It's a first step. It's a beginning.'

I thought again of Nelis's horde of lethal weapons.

'But do you really think that –' I almost said his name – Nelis. Stopped myself in the nick of time. '– any of these gang leaders would just come forward with their guns because there's a gun amnesty?'

'No. it'll take more than a gun amnesty to get the big boys. But it's a beginning.'

I could have told my dad then where Nelis's guns were hidden. Why didn't I? Because it would raise too many questions, like how did I know? Like why hadn't I told him before?

He nudged me. 'You went into one of your wee dreams there. What are you thinking about?' He wanted to talk. I could see that. I think he felt he was doing something at last, instead of just complaining about it. I watched him as he talked on and his voice seemed to fade into the distance. I was hardly listening. All I was thinking was that he was a lot like Armour, my dad. In different ways they were trying to make the town a better place.

'Everybody's got to do their bit,' he was saying. ' "Be the change you want to see in the world." A wise man once said that.' He smiled at me. 'Do you know who that wise man was?'

'My granddad,' I said, grinning back at him. 'He's the

one who usually said the wise things according to you.'

'Not this time. This was Gandhi.'

I hadn't a clue who Gandhi was. And it didn't matter. Because what my dad had said only made me feel better about helping Armour. I was doing my bit too. I was trying to be the change I wanted to see in the world – well in the town anyway. And maybe one day Sean – everybody – would understand.

So I met up with Nelis next day at the pool hall. I think that was his headquarters. And I thought then that Armour had nothing to be afraid of from this creep. Nelis had no presence. No real personality. Not like Armour, who seemed to fill the room with his. Nor did he have any ambition. Not like Armour with his lovely home, his dream of being a legitimate businessman, working to make life better for his family. Armour could have got rid of Nelis with a flick of his finger, like a fly from his hand. I admired the fact he was trying to negotiate a peaceful settlement. It had worked in Ireland after all the fighting, Armour had told me. He wanted to make it work here.

'Tell Armour we have a deal. But on my terms,' Nelis told me. 'And my terms are pretty steep.'

I didn't understand what he meant but Armour did.

He picked me up after the meeting and he was stony-faced when I told him.

'He wants money, Leo. Do you realise that? That creep wants money to move out of town.'

'And are you going to give him money?'

He looked at me for an age. 'If that's what it takes,' he said.

30

Mr Sheridan was all over the front pages of the local paper the next day.

FRAMED?

That was the headline.

He had no alibi for the night of the murder. He'd been heard threatening McCrae. 'I'm gonnae kill you!' He'd said it time and time again. And now, someone had come forward to say they had seen him hanging around McCrae's house that night. Looking suspicious, looking angry.

'Another nail in his coffin,' my dad said as he read the paper. We were sitting at the table having our tea.

'Put that down and eat,' my mum told him. 'You're a bad influence on the boys.' But as soon as he had she added, 'You don't really think it was him, do you?'

My dad started eating his chicken. I held my breath. Stared at him, waiting for his answer. 'Well, he had a perfect motive. Who could blame him?'

'His girl's death tore him apart,' Mum agreed. 'I feel that sorry for him.'

I looked at Mum.

'I still don't think he did it,' Dad said.

My eyes swivelled back to my dad.

'And I'll tell you why. Why should he claim he's being framed?' Dad went on. 'I think he'd be shouting his guilt from the rooftops.'

Now it was my mum's turn. 'But who would be framing him?' I looked back to her. Why couldn't they just stop talking about this!

'I'll give you three guesses,' my dad said. I turned to look at him now. 'Though two might be enough.'

'Armour or Nelis,' my mum said. My head was snapping back and forth like someone at a tennis match. 'But the police must know that.'

'Aye, they'll know – but what proof have they got? What proof do they ever get? When do any of those two ever get caught?'

My mum laughed then. 'Oh well, we've managed to

solve the crime that's been baffling the cops for weeks. We should go into business. A crime-fighting duo?'

Out of the blue my dad announced, 'I'm going to start a petition. Maybe even a march. A lot of people are angry about Sheridan being in jail. About how easily guns are available here. They might be angry enough to do something about it. And if Armour and Nelis see just how many people are against them, they won't think they're God Almighty any more. Neither of them.'

Stop talking about this! I wanted desperately to shout that out at them. But they wouldn't shut up.

'Och, who do you think you are, Dave? Martin-blinking-Luther King?'

My dad smiled then. My mum could always make him smile. I looked at David, sitting across the table from me. My mum noticed him now too.

'What on earth are you doing, David?' Mum asked him.

'Copying Leo. Leo's doing this.' He began turning his head wildly to the left and to the right. So fast that his eyes began to go together and he almost fell off his chair.

We all began to laugh then. In fact, I laughed so hard the bit of chicken lodged in my throat and I was the one

157

who fell off the chair.

But I was laughing with relief. David had got them to stop talking about it. I couldn't bear listening to them for one more minute. I knew I would have to ask Armour when he was going to produce the proof that would free Mr Sheridan.

The only chance I had to phone him was next day on my way to school. I hated talking about it over the phone. Phones could be tapped, he'd told me. His phone especially. So I was careful to cover what I was saying, mentioning no names.

'Leo, I know what you're worried about,' he said when I'd finished. 'You're a good boy thinking like that. How about if I pick you up after school – say, at the Police Club round the corner? And we'll talk about it.'

The day went too slowly. Couldn't concentrate on anything. Sean didn't look my way any more. He seemed to be with Aidan all the time now. Aidan, his best pal? No way, surely. We used to have such a giggle about Aidan. And both of them were always with Veronika and Shannon. They ate with them at lunchtime and sat on the steps with them during break.

Who was my friend now?

I had no one. Except the lowlives in the school. The ones we used to avoid like the plague. They were keen to be my friend now. Now that I was involved with Armour.

But I shunned them too.

I didn't need friends, I decided. I had my mum and dad and David. And once this was over, and Nelis was bought off, there would be peace in the town. And they would learn that Armour wasn't as bad as he was painted.

But later that day, as I stood in the playground, watching Sean and Aidan and Shannon and Veronika all talking and laughing together – yes, even sour-faced Shannon – I would have done anything to be able to cross over to them and join in.

Armour was waiting at the Police Club. Sitting in his car watching for me coming along the quiet street. He leaned over and opened the door for me as I approached him.

The Police Club has nothing to do with the police any longer. Now it's used for dances and weddings and discos but everyone still calls it the Police Club. It stands on a corner, hidden from the view of any houses. Always quiet and deserted during the day. He'd picked a good place to meet. No one could spot his car here. He drove off even before I had a chance to snap on the seatbelt. 'We'll just go for a wee drive.'

The car had smoked-glass windows. No one would even know I was in here. Even Sean's nosy cousin couldn't spot me in here. And all the time he was driving, he reassured me. Any day now he planned to make sure Sheridan was released. He had it all in place. But for the moment he was safer in jail. Some of McCrae's men had sworn they would get him as soon as he stepped back on to the street.

'But once this is settled with Nelis, McCrae's men will know it's finished for them too. And it's going to be finished with Nelis very soon.' He stopped the car on the hill overlooking the town. We were up at the new cemetery – deserted on this cold afternoon.

'I wouldn't mind a plot here,' my granny would say. 'Look at the view I would have.'

And the view was stupendous. From here you could look right down the Clyde where it opened up into the Irish Sea. On this clear, crisp day I could almost see Ailsa Craig, the big island of rock that marked the halfway point between Glasgow and Belfast. 'Paddy's

Milestone', we called it.

Armour stared at it too. Drew in a deep breath of air. 'Look at that view. This town's worth fighting for, isn't it?'

It was how I felt too. How my dad felt. They weren't so different.

'With your help, Leo, we can get this finished.' He hesitated. 'I need to know how much Nelis wants.'

I was watching a boat gliding down the river, cutting it like glass. 'You want me to meet him again?'

'One last time, I promise.'

'I've heard that before,' I said.

But I was in too deep to say no. Didn't want to anyway. In that moment, I knew I didn't want to. 'When and where?' I asked.

He smiled at me. 'Just like that. When and where? You're some boy, Leo. Cool as they make them.'

The boat's horn sounded on the river. Armour started up the engine again. 'Do you know something, Leo? One day you could be The Man.'

31

I could be The Man. I couldn't get those words out of my head all that night. *I could be The Man.*

Taking over. In charge. People listened to Armour. People stepped back to let him pass.

I imagined myself in his place. Taking over. Ordering men around. Seeing them move aside when I approached.

It was happening already. At school when I walked into the playground they would watch me. They would move to let me pass.

Did I change then? Or had I already changed? I don't know. But next day when I went to school I felt different. Not alone any more.

But apart.

Like Armour said – when you're The Man, you've got to keep friends at arm's length. Not let anyone get

162

too close. I liked the way I felt that day.

I was to meet Nelis the next day. Only this time it was to be in town, in full view of everyone. It was to look like a chance meeting – an accident. I was going to bump into him in Tesco's. And this time it was me who arranged it all. A simple text message to Nelis's mobile.

4pm Tuesday. Tescos. Cakes.

Couldn't sound more innocent.

An undercover operation, that's what it felt like. And I was excited at the thought of it. It was the kind of thing Sean and I used to love pretending to do. A game we loved acting out.

Sean.

I pushed him to the back of my mind. He was the past. This was now.

All I needed was an excuse to go to Tesco's. Let's face it, me in Tesco's would set Mum's alarm bells ringing right off.

Then my dad solved it all with his petition. He was all talk of it at teatime.

'I've put one in each shop in the area. I went into

Mr Brown's and every customer in the shop signed up right away. That's how desperate people are to get rid of guns.'

My mum chimed in. 'Give me one. I'll get them to sign it at the hospital.'

A bulb switched on above my head. 'I'll hand one into Tesco's for you. Tomorrow after school.'

My dad beamed at me. 'Good thinking, Leo.'

Did I feel guilty about that?

No. I felt good. Good and clever. Clever enough to find a perfect cover for my meeting with Nelis.

First thing I did when I went into Tesco's was hand in the petition. Dad was right, they seemed eager to get it. One of the smaller Tesco's on the road out of town had been held up last week at gunpoint. The manager told me they were going to photocopy the petition and put it at the end of every checkout.

Then I lifted a basket and sauntered round the store.

Cakes and biscuits – Armour had liked that. 'Suits him. He's nothing but a fairy cake anyway. And past his sell-by date.'

I wasn't even afraid of Nelis any more. Though his reputation was vile. Nelis seemed weak and insignificant to me now. Not like Armour at all. Armour wanted him out of town. But he wasn't threatening violence. He was willing to pay to get him out. Give him money to go.

I picked up a choc ice and a couple of packets of sweets. Not Mint Imperials – I couldn't look at them now without feeling sick – and I headed for the cake aisle.

I saw him right off, at the other end of the aisle. Pretending an interest in home baking. But he'd seen me too, though he didn't look my way. He began to move, step by step, in my direction.

My heart didn't beat any faster at the sight of him. I wasn't afraid. I wasn't even nervous. If anything I was excited. I was determined to do this right. And this was going to be the tricky bit. Trying to make our collision look natural.

One more step. I could reach out and touch him if I wanted but I didn't. Instead I swung round. My basket caught on his jacket. I let it drop. He stumbled.

He was all apologies. 'Sorry, son. Sorry. Here, let me get them.' He bent to pick up the sweets. So did I.

As we crouched together he smiled at me. He had a tooth missing. I had never noticed that before.

'Here, son – tell Armour I don't come cheap. This is

my price.' The price he mentioned almost made me fall back on the floor. 'Not a penny less. No negotiation. OK? And he'll get what he wants.'

I said nothing. Just took the packet from him and stood up.

'No worries,' was all I said.

I walked away and all I could think was how well I had carried it off. Anyone watching would have seen an accidental collision. Nothing more.

'Here, son, wait a minute.'

I froze. Nelis calling me back. It had all gone so well. What was he doing?

I turned and he was walking towards me. 'Here, you nearly forgot your choc ice.'

And he dropped it in the basket and walked on.

32

I sent a text to Armour with the price Nelis had mentioned. That was all. He would know what it meant.

Would Armour be able to pay that much money? And was it just to get Nelis out of town? He would only move somewhere else, wouldn't he? Start all over again. Or was the payment to stop all his drug dealing, his violence? And could he be trusted? Armour was too clever to let Nelis fool him.

'He's the dangerous one,' Armour had told me. And didn't I know it? Hadn't I found his hoard of guns? 'But he's greedy too. He'll take the money.'

If Armour had been there with me at that moment I would have told him about them. About the guns. I realised how much I wanted to talk to him. Tell him how Nelis had looked, tell him all that happened. A step-by-step account.

But this was nothing that I could talk about

over the phone.

I crossed into Boots, had a look at the perfumes. Mum's birthday was coming up. I walked with a real spring in my step. I'd read that once in a book and had thought it was the daftest way I'd ever heard to describe how someone walked. Now I realised exactly what it meant. I bounced with confidence. I had carried an important message for The Man. I was trusted.

One day I might even be The Man myself.

I didn't feel like a boy any more. Remembering the games I had played with Sean – C.S.I. investigators, detectives, commandos – they all seemed juvenile and silly now.

The games I played now were for real.

Armour called me next day. To congratulate me. Thank me for all my hard work. 'If all this works out, it'll be all down to you. Do you know that?'

I felt a pride rise in me. All down to me. 'Are you going to pay him?'

'What do you think? Is it too much?'

He was asking me! 'It's a lot of money,' I said. 'Have you got that kind of money?'

He didn't answer that. All he said was, 'If it gets us what we want I'm willing to pay.'

If it gets us – *us* what we want? He was including me in all this.

'How do you know you can trust him?'

I could hear the smile in Armour's voice. 'If you were in my shoes . . . how would *you* make sure you could trust him, Leo?'

I thought about it. 'I'd have something in place, something of his that I could use to make sure he doesn't change his mind. Insurance.'

I'd seen that once in a TV detective series. Armour obviously hadn't seen the same programme. He thought it was all my idea.

'You are one clever boy, Leo. That's exactly what I have in mind too. If he tries to go back on his word . . . I have insurance too.'

I should have known he would.

'I'm going to think about this, Leo. Then maybe you'll set up the meeting. Would you do that?'

Me? Set up the meeting that would get rid of Nelis, maybe bring peace to the town?

'Yes,' I said.

'How am I ever going to thank you for all this, Leo?'

But I didn't need his thanks any more. I was doing this because I wanted to.

I hardly noticed Sean and Veronika when they passed me in the corridor that day. They hardly looked at me anyway. It was as if we'd never been friends. I was a world away from Sean now.

Dad came in from work that night and I could see right off he had a spring in his step too.

He had flowers for Mum and handed them to her and kissed her.

'Wow! What's happened to you?' she asked him.

He looked around at us. I was at the table helping David with his homework. He beamed a big smile at us.

'I've got another job. In electronics. The job I nearly had a few weeks ago, remember? Well the guy who got the job let them down. I was next in line. I've got it. More money. Permanent job. Exactly what I wanted.'

His voice was excited. Mum ran at him and threw her arms around him. David grabbed the opportunity to escape his homework and ran and jumped on top of them both.

Me, I just sat there thinking.

My dad had a better job.

How am I ever going to thank you? Armour had asked.

What better way than this? My dad had the job he'd always wanted.

My mum noticed my silence then. 'Nothing to say, Leo? How about, "That's brilliant, Dad."'

She was watching me, so was Dad.

'It is. It's brilliant, Dad. It's just . . . such a surprise.'

'When did you find out?' Mum asked him. 'You didn't get any letters this morning.'

'A phone call,' Dad explained. 'Today at lunchtime. Out of the blue. Can you believe it?'

I didn't listen to the rest of what he was saying. I didn't need to.

When I spoke to him on the way to school this morning, Armour had asked me 'How am I ever going to thank you?' And by lunchtime, he had figured out how to thank me. Set the wheels in motion.

Quick work.

He really was The Man.

'Seems to me,' Dad said, when he'd finally settled down to have his tea, 'that this family has a lot to be thankful for.'

It was only later he remembered his other news, driven to the back of his mind by the more important matter of his new job. 'By the way, I was interviewed by the paper this afternoon. About the petition. I'm going to be on the front page tomorrow.'

33

I wanted to thank Armour. I had to thank him. This was the job my dad had dreamed of. Wanted so badly. Back at his trade. Big money.

Did I dare go to his house again?

In the end all I did was text him.

Thanks

He would know what I meant.

He called me, as he usually did now, on my way to school next morning. I always walked past the Police Club – discreet, isolated – to wait for his call.

'I've decided I'm going to pay him. But this time we have to meet. Face to face.'

He didn't even have to ask me this time. 'I'll go to the pool hall after school. Bet he'll be there.'

'Bet he will,' Armour said, with a smile in his voice. 'You be careful, Leo.'

I promised him I would. 'Did you get my text?'

'You're thanking me enough,' he said. 'Doing all this for me.'

'But that new job. That's the one Dad really wanted. I don't know how you managed it so quickly.'

There was a long pause on the line. So long that for a moment I thought we'd been cut off.

'Oh, that,' he said at last. 'That was nothing.'

I laughed. 'Nothing to you. A lot to my dad.'

'Well you set this up and we're even.'

I would set it up – and I'd do it well. It was all I thought about that day. Meeting Nelis, asking him to name a date, a place, hoping that Armour could trust him. I thought of nothing else.

Even when Aidan actually spoke to me in the corridor it hardly registered. 'Looks like your best pal's stolen your girl,' he sneered. And he nodded in the direction of Sean and Veronika. They were standing together, laughing. Together so often these days I realised. Sean and Veronika. Had he always fancied her? Was our fight just an excuse for him to move right in?

I'd always thought it would be Aidan she'd go off

with. By the bitterness in his voice – and the look on his face – so did Aidan.

'Jealous, Aidan?' I asked him.

'Not half as jealous as you must be.' And he moved away from me.

I wouldn't care about it, I thought. Wouldn't think about it. I had enough on my mind.

Nelis was slumped in a chair at the pool hall, flanked by two of the hooded lowlives who were supposed to be his bodyguards. He stood up when he saw me coming.

'Ah, here comes my ticket to the big money.'

'Armour says just name the place and the date and he'll meet you.'

'Hear that, boys? Armour needs Nelis, eh?' His mouth widened in a smile. He shouldn't even try to smile, I thought. His teeth were so badly stained with nicotine. 'Let's make it next Sunday morning. 3 a.m. We don't want any witnesses, do we?'

'Where?' I asked him.

'My turf,' he said. 'Up at the old Willow Bar. And tell him to come alone. He brings anybody with him and the deal's off.'

The old Willow Bar. How often had Sean and I

explored in that place? It was supposed to be haunted. Haunted by the ghost of a man who'd been shot in there. Nelis had been behind that shooting. Everyone knew it. His men had rushed in when the place had been crowded and sprayed the place with bullets. The man who died was a complete innocent. Caught in the crossfire. Because of that shooting, customers had stayed away. The Willow Bar had eventually closed down. No surprise there. You don't go out for a quiet drink and expect a battalion of gunmen to rush in and blast you to kingdom come.

I sent a text to Armour as I was walking home. Telling him the where and when. Added:

B careful

Nelis was dangerous. Nelis had guns. A whole stash of them in fact. Clyde Terrace was only a street away from the Willow Bar. Could Nelis be trusted? What if he couldn't? I should tell Armour about the guns. But it wasn't something I could text, or even say over the phone. I'd have to wait until I saw him.

I had forgotten all about my dad's interview until I got home.

Mum had pinned the newspaper up on the wall in the kitchen. A photo of him was splashed across the front page holding up his petition. The headline:

NO MORE GUNS

'He'll do it,' my mum said. 'I've never known your dad to start anything he didn't finish.'

The phone kept ringing all night. People congratulating Dad – people wanting to help. Even the town Provost phoned to ask what he could do. I could see my dad swell with pride with every call. He was doing something at last.

I was up in my bedroom reading when the phone rang again. David was in his room – supposed to be sleeping, but I could hear him on his Nintendo. Dad dived for the phone, his feet skidding across the hall. Didn't want it to wake David, on the remote chance he might be asleep.

I heard the low murmur of his voice downstairs, then growing louder. 'Who is that? *Who is that?*'

I don't think he got an answer. The next thing his feet were bounding noisily upstairs, not caring how loud he was now. That should have warned me.

The door of my room was flung open with such force it banged against the wall and flew back. My dad was standing there – his face purple with rage.

'What is it?' I asked. Yet somehow I already knew.

'I've just had a phone call to say I've got some nerve trying to clean up this town when my son runs messages for Armour.'

34

My dad grabbed me by the shoulders, lifted me from the chair. My dad – who hardly ever lost his temper – was scaring me.

'Tell me it's not true. Tell me . . . and I'll believe you.'

I wanted to lie but I couldn't find the words.

He looked puzzled, as if he didn't recognise me. 'It's not true. You're too sensible. You know how bad this guy is.'

My mouth was so dry I could hardly get the words out. 'Maybe . . . he's not as bad as you think.'

If I'd slapped him he couldn't have looked more shocked.

'Not as bad as I *think*! Are we talking about the same person? Armour? He's a loan shark, a drug dealer. He gets people beaten up, he's been up for murder . . . *that* Armour? And you're saying . . . he's not as bad as I think? What planet are you on, Leo?'

By this time, my mum had flown upstairs too. Her face was white. 'Leo, how did you get involved with Armour?'

How could I tell her, explain to either of them? 'I'm not involved with him. I've met him, that's all.'

My dad turned to Mum. 'He runs messages for him.' He dropped me and ran his hands through his hair. 'I can't believe this is happening. A man on the phone there, telling me my son runs messages for Armour. He's Armour's boy, he said.'

I decided to get angry then. 'And you believe somebody on the phone and not me?'

My dad looked deep into my eyes. 'Tell me it's not true. I'll believe you. You don't know how much I want this to be a lie.'

'How did you meet him, Leo?' my mum said softly. Not wanting it to be true either.

My brain was desperately trying to come up with an answer that sounded credible. 'It was an accident. I bumped into him. He was nice – he seemed OK.'

'I was told you've been to his house,' my dad said.

'Once,' I said, and in that moment it came to me what I could tell them. A believable reason. 'The day I bumped into him I was getting chased by the Bissett

Boys. He got them off my back. I wanted to thank him.'

'Why would he do that for you? He's not exactly Santa Claus.'

I had given him a good reason and he still didn't believe me. I couldn't argue any more. So I got angry too. 'What does it matter? He helped me. The Bissett Boys don't bother me any more.'

'Why would he do that for you, Leo?' My dad's anger was gone – what took its place was something much more scary. 'Why would he do that for you?' he asked me again, his voice cold.

Thinking fast was becoming easier. 'He knows how bad the Bissett Boys are. And since then they've never chased me again. I went to his house to say thanks. That's all.'

'And that makes him a good guy?' He shook his head. 'How could you be so stupid, Leo?' He stepped forward so quickly, I thought he was going to hit me. My dad, who had never lifted a hand to me. I should have known better. 'Well, I'm telling you now, Leo – you will never see him again, talk to him again, have anything to do with him again. Do you hear me?

My mum laid a hand on his arm, as if she was holding him back, but her eyes were on me. Angry eyes. She seemed to draw him from the room.

My stomach had curled into a steel ball. I listened hard, trying to hear what they were saying but I couldn't make out their words. I could only sense the anger, disappointment, hurt. Then – I don't know how much later – the front door slammed and Dad's car revved up. I heard him roaring off into the night. No prizes for guessing where he was going. To Armour's house. To warn him off. To tell him to keep his hands off his son.

I had to get to Armour first. Let him know my dad was on his way. Tell him not to hurt my dad.

I went into the bathroom and locked the door – didn't want my mum walking in on me – and I called Armour.

He answered almost at once. Must have seen my number and wondered why I was calling him so late. 'Leo,' he said. 'Something's wrong.'

I tried to speak calmly. Not let the words come out in a nervous tumble. 'Somebody called my dad. Told him I was running for you.'

'Who called him?'

'I don't know. Doesn't matter. But he's raging. Made me swear not to see you again. He's on his way to your place. Please, don't do anything to him.'

'Leo! Me. Do something to your dad? How could I

do anything to him? Anyway, I'm finished with all that, I told you. I'll talk to him.'

'I told him you got the Bissett Boys off my back. That I only went to your house the once to thank you.'

'I'll back you up, Leo.' His voice was reassuring. 'You told him nothing about Nelis – about our little deal?'

'You know I wouldn't do that,' I said.

'I know. And don't worry about your dad. I'll handle him.'

I don't know what was said that night. Dad came back two hours later and went straight to bed. In the morning he came into my room before he set off for work. He looked as if he hadn't slept all night. 'I've told Armour to keep well away from you. And you keep well away from him. I'm not going to tell you again, Leo.'

'OK,' I said.

Dad sat on the bed beside me. 'I still can't get over you going to this man's house, Leo.'

I tried to say something, but he held up his hand to stop me. 'No, Leo. People like Armour are devious. They never do anything without an ulterior motive. It worries me what his might be.'

'He's not got an ulterior motive, Dad –'

But he wouldn't listen.

'People like him are like vampires. They like to bleed people dry – bleed boys like you dry. And once they've got their teeth into you, son . . . they never let go.'

'I'm not daft, Dad.'

He looked at me in a way I'd never seen him look at me before, as if he was trying to fathom if he could really believe that. 'I hope not, Leo. I've always been able to trust you. Don't let me down.'

He stood up.

'But this has done one thing. It's made me more determined than ever to get rid of people like him from this town. Because if my son can even *begin* to think Armour's decent, how easily can any other boy be fooled by him? I'm not going to stop till I get rid of them all.'

I wasn't being fooled by Armour. I so wanted to tell Dad everything then – what Armour had done for us and how little he had asked in return. But I knew he wouldn't listen. He wouldn't believe that Armour wanted the same thing he did. He wanted the town clean and safe. But it wasn't the time.

He'd know soon enough, I promised myself. Then my dad would understand.

35

Over the next couple of days Dad redoubled his efforts with the petition. He was at the police station regularly, checking what else could be done.

I was convinced he'd told the police about the call and me being involved with Armour. Every time I passed a policeman in the street I felt he would look at me as if he knew I was Armour's boy. And that made me angry too. As if I'd done something wrong. When all I'd done right from the beginning was try to protect my family, my best friend.

No. Wipe that. I had no best friend now. Sean seemed like a distant memory. The whispered giggles in the school were all about Sean and Veronika. Always together.

As for my family, the only one who seemed to appreciate me – the only one I could still talk to – was David, and he was only five.

'Why's my dad mad at you?' he kept asking. 'You been bad?'

'No, I have not!' I would always reply. 'I've been really good. It's not fair.'

Then he'd sit close beside me and whisper, 'I know you've been good. You're the best big brother in the world.'

But as for my mum and dad, the atmosphere with them was icy. Mum dropped me off at school and picked me up, hardly saying a word to me. She had to juggle her hours at the hospital to keep her eye on me, she said. And it was a good thing she was on flexitime. They were both making sure I didn't see Armour again.

They couldn't stop the calls, though. Didn't know about them.

Armour called me every day. Now that my mum took me to school he would usually call me during my lunch break. I asked him what had happened when my dad came to the house, but all he would say was that he'd backed me up.

'The boy only wanted to thank me. Those Bissett Boys are a bad lot. They needed warning off,' he'd said to my dad, but to me he'd added, 'I don't know why your dad didn't stop them himself, Leo.'

Those words had stayed with me all that day. Why *hadn't* my dad done anything to stop the Bissett Boys? He knew what they were like and what they were doing and he'd done nothing to help me. It had taken Armour to get them off my back. Now it was the Bissett Boys who were afraid of me.

Dad started his new job. Mum said I'd taken the joy out of it for him. Trying to make me feel guilty. He was so worried about me, she said. I wanted to scream at her, *It's thanks to me he's got the job. Me – and Armour!*

If only Armour would prove to my dad he'd turned into one of the good guys. It would come soon. The deal with Nelis would show that. I only had to wait a few days and then it would all come right.

Nelis. Out of the picture. Moved away from this town maybe.

Then there was the gun amnesty. If people handed in their guns there would be no comeback to them. No charges. That was another moment when I almost told Armour about the guns I'd found. If Armour was the one who told the police about them – handed them in himself – he'd prove he'd turned over a new leaf.

I could almost see the headlines.

ARMOUR HANDS IN NELIS ARSENAL

But that would be grassing and I had a feeling he wouldn't do that. Better this way. It would all be done without any fighting.

My dad and Armour were on the same side. I pictured them getting to know each other. Saw them standing face to face, shaking hands. Not becoming friends, never that. But maybe coming to realise that they each wanted the same thing . . . what was best for the town. Then my dad would know that I had done the right thing.

'Is it all still on for Sunday?' I asked him one day. 'Once it's done, my dad will get off my back.'

'Sunday. 3 a.m.,' he told me. 'Thanks to you. You'll never know how much you've helped me, Leo.'

'I wish you could tell my dad that. I want him to understand what you're trying to do.'

I could hear him laughing. 'I wish you could tell him to keep things down a bit till this deal's done. His petition – all this publicity he's getting. It's making Nelis really nervous. I don't want it to fall through because of your dad.'

Now I was the one who was nervous. 'You think it might because of my dad?'

'I hope not, Leo. If he could back down a bit, it would be great. But it's all going to work out. You'll see.' He paused. 'And your dad will be the first one to know about it. I promise.'

After that, I found I was getting annoyed at my dad. Annoyed every time he mentioned the petition, the amnesty, his visits to the police. I wanted to shut him up, till this deal was done. Till Nelis had his money and was gone. Dad didn't understand anything. He hadn't helped me against the Bissett Boys. His petition would do no good. The amnesty would do no good. Get a few guns off the street, that was all.

Only Armour could do things right.

Only Armour could get things done.

36

It was all coming to a head. I could feel it. Dad was angry at me. I was angry at Dad. The atmosphere in the house was awful. I didn't want him to talk to me about Armour, and I knew he was bursting to talk to me about him.

It would only take one little thing for the tension to break to the surface. And the little thing was Sean.

Friday teatime, and Dad came in after his first week in his new job with a present for Mum. A pair of earrings.

'Anything for me, Dad?' David wanted a present too. As if Dad would ever forget him. He'd bought him a new game for his Nintendo. I didn't ask for a present but he hadn't left me out. 'Here.' He threw a book at me. 'Heard you saying you wanted to read that.'

I began to say a stumbling 'thank you', but he had

something else on his mind. 'I met Sean in the town,' he said. 'You remember you used to be friendly with him?'

I flicked through the book, biting at the inside of my mouth. Said nothing.

'I asked him if he knew about you and Armour.'

I snapped the book shut. He'd never let it go.

'He didn't know anything, he said. Till he heard about it at school. Seems it was all over the school. Seems it was only your daft old dad that didn't know.'

He was waiting for me to say something but still I kept my mouth shut.

'And it seems it wasn't just that one wee visit you made to his house to thank him.' His voice grew angry. 'What a liar you are, boy.'

My mum stepped between us then. 'Dave, calm down.'

He motioned her aside. 'No, I have to know this. How often have you seen him? What have you been doing for him?'

Finally I spoke, my voice as angry as his. 'Did Sean tell you all this?'

'Sean? Your pal, Sean? The one you ditched for Armour? No. Sean wouldn't say a word against you. It was his mate Aidan who told me.'

'Typical Aidan,' I snapped. 'Doesn't know how to keep his trap shut.'

'You better tell me everything, Leo. Right now. I want to hear the truth.'

My mum slipped her arm around David's shoulders. 'Come on, you come and help me with the tea, David.'

I stood up. I felt I didn't belong in this family any more. I was an outsider.

'I'm waiting, Leo.'

'You think Armour's so bad. Well, he's never done anything bad to me. Only good things.'

Dad gripped me by the shoulders. 'And what exactly are you doing for Armour?'

I knew what he was thinking. That I was carrying drugs for him. How I wished then that I could tell him the truth. That what I was doing for him was a good thing.

'He's never asked me to do anything bad for him. He's not the bad guy you think he is.'

'He's a villain! Leo, when did you stop believing that?'

He grabbed me by the shoulders, gripping so hard it hurt. I shook myself away from him. 'If only you knew . . . if only you knew . . .'

191

'If only I knew what?'

I didn't want to tell him. Why was he making me tell him? 'You should be grateful to Armour.' I started shouting. 'He's done plenty for you!'

Dad stepped back then. Shock on his face. 'He's done plenty for me? What's Armour ever done for me?'

I didn't answer him. I wanted him to let it go. But he wouldn't.

'Tell me! Why would Armour do anything for me?'

'To thank me. To help me. He likes me. I think he's the only one who does.'

'You better tell me what this is all about, Leo. And don't lie. I want to know the truth.'

He wanted the truth? Well, he was going to get it.

I knew what I was about to say was going to hurt him – more painfully than a knife in his back. And I didn't care. 'You think Armour's so bad? Well, you wouldn't have a job if it wasn't for him. He got you them both. He talked to the right people, made a few phone calls, and you got your job the next day.'

He let me go. Those words were like a slap in the face. My mum must have been listening to everything. She pushed the door open and came running in.

'I don't believe that,' she shouted at me. 'Armour's

not the type to do anybody any favours.'

'Well, he did it,' I yelled back. 'And you should be grateful to him.'

I was out of the house and running before they could stop me. I was going to Armour's house. It seemed like a haven now. I would go to him and tell him about Nelis's stash of guns, let him take the glory for getting rid of guns in the town. Not my dad. And once he did, my mum and my dad would really know the truth. Armour wasn't so bad.

I was Armour's boy . . . and I was proud of it.

37

I thought they might have run out after me. But no one came. The front door stayed shut. That's how much they cared, I thought.

I backed towards the end of the street, still expecting my dad to come flying after me any moment. What I'd said must have hurt him. But who could blame me? He should have just let it go, not go on and on about Armour the way he had.

No one came after me. I stood for a moment watching the house, wondering what was happening inside. Half of me hoping Mum or Dad would appear at the front door, urge me back. But no one came. I turned at last, not looking where I was going. Didn't see the figure who leaped out in front of me from the bushes.

The face terrified me. It was out of shape, discoloured. The eyes had almost disappeared inside dark blue bulges. The cheeks were swollen, the face bruised and blackened and bloody. Did I know him? Would I recognise him if I did? I didn't think so. He didn't even look human.

The man grabbed me by the shoulders, almost spat at me. 'Not too pretty, eh?' He could hardly speak clearly. I could see some of his teeth were missing too. 'This is thanks to you, wee man.'

I squirmed to get away from him. 'Me?'

'You told him I was the one who phoned your dad, didn't ye?'

What was he talking about?

'Armour.' He pointed to his face as if it wasn't part of him any more, but a specimen in a jar. 'This! His boys came for me 'cause I told your dad about you.'

I was shaking my head, desperate to be free of him, not wanting to believe what he was saying. 'How could I know it was you?'

Was he crying? Or were his swollen eyes just watering? I could hardly see his eyes.

'No. Maybe not. You cannae hide from Armour. Armour knows everything.' He glanced around as if someone might be watching him from the trees, from the bushes. It was then I realised just how alone we were, here on the deserted street. The man dragged me closer. Too close. I could see the spittle round his lips. I was afraid of what he was going to do. He wanted to hurt me. I knew he wanted to hurt me.

'Wish I had the nerve,' he said, as if he'd been reading my mind. 'The nerve to batter you the way he got me battered.' His voice broke. 'But I'm no' evil like Armour.'

He almost threw me away from him. 'I'm getting out of this toon. Might be safe somewhere else. Got to get away from Armour.'

I couldn't answer him. Because all this didn't seem real. As if it was happening to someone else.

He began to stumble back down the street. I wanted to shout after him, that he was wrong. He was making a mistake. Armour wouldn't do that to him. Armour had changed. He was finished with violence. He was trying to make peace. To become respectable. It couldn't have been Armour.

Because if it was . . . that meant he had lied to me . . . and, why would he lie to me?

I had to see him. I had to find out. The world was upside down.

38

It was his wife who opened the door. She didn't look surprised to see me. She held the door wide.

'He's in there.' She nodded to the front room. 'But he's busy. You better wait here.'

Then she walked back into the kitchen and closed the door. I was alone in the hall. There was a chair against the wall, but I couldn't sit down. I paced back and forth like one of the tigers you see at the zoo. Locked in a cage, looking for a way out. That man had to have been lying. Armour was finished with violence. He wanted to go legitimate. It had been one of his men, I had decided. One of his men had beaten the man up thinking he was doing Armour some kind of favour.

But how had they found out that was the man who'd called my dad?

Armour knows everything.

That was the thought that leaped into my mind. I pushed it out again. Armour wouldn't do that. Not now.

It was still light, the setting sun flooding the hallway through the glass door. The only sound I could hear was the ticking of the clock on the wall, its pendulum swaying back and forth. Ten past seven. Today was Friday. On Sunday at three in the morning, Armour was meeting Nelis. And then my dad would learn the truth. He'd be the first to know – Armour had promised me. The clock was ticking the minutes away till then.

The front-room door was open slightly. And I could only hear the murmur of voices – men's voices – in there.

Then Armour's voice rose above the rest. Confident. In charge. I had to hear what he was saying. I moved closer to the door and listened. He was talking about Nelis.

'By this time next week Nelis will be finished. Out of here. I'm going to make sure of it . . .'

I felt relief flood over me. I had a silent conversation with my dad. As if he was there in front of me. *See, he's doing what he said. What you want to do. He's getting rid of Nelis.*

He hadn't lied to me.

Armour went on talking. 'By this time next week.

Nelis will be in the nick.'

I thought I'd heard him wrong for a second. In the nick? I moved even closer to the door.

'On Sunday, I'll find out where those guns of his are – where he's stashed them. When I've done that . . . a wee phone call to the cops, they find the guns, arrest Nelis . . . and bye bye Nelis.'

'Would it not be better to get the guns for yourself?' a wary voice asked. Not used to questioning the boss.

'That's what Nelis thinks. That I want to buy his stupid guns. Well, I don't need them. I've got guns,' Armour snapped. 'And I can get more any time I want. What I want is to get rid of Nelis. No Nelis. No McCrae. Only one man left standing. Me. The Man, taking over the whole show.'

I still didn't want to believe what I was hearing. He was trying to sound hard in front of his men. Didn't want any of them to think he was going soft. That was it. Had to be.

Because I couldn't bear the alternative.

Armour was going to grass on Nelis.

I'd been used. Duped. Willing to do anything because I was sure he only wanted what my dad wanted. Peace.

But why would he lie to me? I still couldn't under-stand that. He hadn't needed me at all. He could have got any of his henchmen to do his running. To be his go-between.

Why me?

No. There had to be more. Something he wasn't telling them – something he *would* tell me.

He couldn't appear weak in their eyes. They couldn't know till the last moment the real deal he was making with Nelis. Couldn't know he wanted to go straight – legitimate.

I still believed him. I had to.

They were leaving. I stepped back in the hallway, back against a table. Knocked over some stupid orna-ment. It crashed to the ground, shattered into pieces. Amour pulled the door open when he heard the noise, started in shock when he saw me. He hadn't expected me. His surprise only lasted for a second. His face broke into a welcoming smile and the famous wink.

'Leo, son, what are you doing here? Wait in the front room for me. Forget the ornament. Cheap tat the wife bought in Benidorm.'

I stood in the front room waiting for him. I was trying to think straight, but I was confused and scared.

I needed to sort things out in my head and didn't have time.

He saw the other men out and then he came back and stood in the doorway, seemed to fill it with his presence. That's what he had. Presence. Even with his shirt open at the neck, his sleeves rolled up high, he looked in charge. He looked like The Man.

He closed the door and came towards me. 'Now what's the problem?'

'It's my dad,' I said. 'He's giving me a hard time.'

'Have a seat. Want something to drink?'

I shook my head. Sat on the arm of a chair. 'I need my dad to know you're doing the right thing. That you're getting rid of Nelis.'

'You'll have to be patient, Leo.'

'My dad's not patient,' I said.

'Maybe you should tell your dad it would be in his best interests to be patient.' He dropped ice into a glass and the sound was a clatter, rat-a-tat-tat. Reminding me of something. Mint Imperials tumbling to the pavement on a quiet street.

'What do you mean, his best interests?'

'Your dad could ruin everything, Leo. I told you – he's making Nelis very nervous.'

'You're still getting rid of Nelis? That's still the plan, isn't it?'

He turned to me now, his glass in his hand. The amber liquid catching the light. 'You know I am. I'm meeting him Sunday morning. The Willow Bar. You made the arrangements.'

I took a deep breath. I had to know. 'You said . . . I heard you saying there . . . he'd be in the nick. This time next week, you said Nelis would be in the nick . . . that as soon as you knew where his guns were you were going to call the police. Tell them about the guns. But I know –'

If he'd hesitated for just a second, if he'd let me go on, I would have explained that I knew exactly what he meant by that. That I knew he'd had to say that to his men – couldn't let them think he'd gone soft. Another second in fact, and I would have told him exactly where Nelis had hidden those guns. He wouldn't even have had to meet him.

But Armour didn't give me that second. His eyes became as cold as the ice in his glass.

'Oh, Leo, why did you have to hear all that?'

39

'I was outside. I couldn't help it.' My mouth was dry. 'I don't understand –'

'Come on, Leo. You're a smart boy. You weren't born yesterday. You knew what we were doing.'

Armour's words were freezing my bones. I laced my fingers together nervously. 'You said you wanted rid of Nelis.'

'And I will be getting rid of Nelis. He'll be in jail. Isn't that what your dad wants too?'

He was confusing me. I couldn't think straight. 'And you . . . you're going to go straight from now on?' I wanted him so much to say that he was. That I'd been right about him. I prayed for those words to come out of his mouth.

He leaned towards me. There was a smile on his face. 'What do you think?'

And I knew then what he had always intended. He'd been planning all along to take over. Be the Number One, the kingpin, The Man.

And I had helped him. 'But you told me –'

He didn't let me finish. '– what you wanted to hear, wee man.'

'I wouldn't have talked to Nelis if I'd known. I wouldn't have helped you.'

'You think I didn't know that?'

And I still didn't understand why he'd needed me, involved me. I was too stupid to understand. 'All that talk about trust – it was rubbish. You didn't trust me. You could have used anybody.'

He sat across from me. 'Not actually true,' he said. 'I knew I could trust you. You'd proved that you knew how to keep your mouth shut.'

'So would anybody else. They'd be too afraid to talk.' So I asked again. 'Why me?'

He drew out a long sigh. 'It doesn't matter now. It'll be over soon. You don't ever have to see me again.'

I jumped to my feet. 'It'll never be over. You used me. You said you wanted the same thing as my dad.'

'And I do. We both want rid of Nelis.'

'My dad wants rid of you too.'

'Ah, that's where we part company, isn't it? And that's where the trouble begins. Because now you know the truth, Leo, I'm warning you – you better call your dad off. When Nelis is out of the picture I want your dad off my back.'

And his words came back to me. *Your dad will be the first to know.* I understood them now, and they chilled me.

'You're warning *me*?' That almost made me laugh. Because that was the second when I realised he couldn't threaten me. I knew too much. Had he forgotten that? 'You leave my dad out of this. Or else.'

What gave me the courage to say such a thing? To Armour? Yet I wasn't scared. I was the one with the power now. I was sure of it.

Armour smiled. Not that disarming smile he'd used on me before – the kind I couldn't help but answer with a smile of my own – but a slow, snarl of a smile that crawled across his face.

And then I *was* scared.

'Or else what, Leo?'

I tried to keep my voice from shaking. 'You know what else. I can still tell the police what I saw. I'm an eyewitness.'

Unless – the sudden thought leaped at me – unless he pulled out a gun and shot me right there. Then I'd be a dead eyewitness.

'They'll ask why you didn't go to the police before.'

Easy answer. 'I'm only a boy. I was scared of you. The police would understand that. Anyone would.'

'But you didn't just not go to the police, Leo. You came to my house. You helped me. You met Nelis for me. Made arrangements for me. You even sent a text to Nelis on your own phone. Hardly the sign of someone who was afraid of me.'

I was trying desperately to think of an answer to that. 'But – but –'

'But nothing, Leo. You talked to Nelis for me. You ran my errands. You accepted my favours. My friend-ship. Everyone knows you were Armour's boy. You, Leo, are an accessory after the fact.'

And now I knew at last why he'd needed me as his go-between.

He *had* used me. Duped me. Reeled me in like a fish on the end of a line.

'They'll put you in borstal, Leo. Your dad's campaign won't look so good when his son is charged as an acces-sory to murder.'

'My dad won't care.' I was yelling now. 'My dad only cares about the truth.'

Armour shrugged. 'Oh well, you know him better than I do.'

Surely though I had something I could use against him? 'I could go to the police, tell them what you plan to do to Nelis.'

But he had an answer for that too. 'Yes, you could. But you know –' He smiled, hesitated for just a moment before he spoke again. 'I've been thinking about that lovely wee brother of yours – David, isn't it? I wonder if he cares about the truth as much as you or your dad?'

That was like a blade in my side. A picture flashed in front of my eyes. The man I'd met on the road, his face swollen and bloody. 'You leave my wee brother out of this! Are you threatening my wee brother!' I screamed the words out at him. I'd kill him myself if he was.

He only looked puzzled. As if he honestly didn't understand what I meant. 'Not at all, Leo. You do what you think is right. I'm sure you'll make the right decision.'

His wife opened the door then. She'd obviously heard my yelling. 'Is everything all right here?'

Would she believe me if I told her? Would she help

me? Would she care? Somehow, I didn't think so.

'Leo's just leaving, honey,' Armour said. 'I'll see him out.'

I yelled at him for one last time. 'I don't need you to see me anywhere.'

Armour raised his arms as if he was surrendering. 'You're the boss, Leo.' And he winked at me. And that was the worst part. That wink. Making a fool of me, of everything I had believed I'd been doing. And I was helpless to do anything.

I wasn't the boss.

There was only one boss.

And it was Armour.

40

I spewed up as soon as I left his house. As soon as I turned the corner out of his sight. I wouldn't let him see me being sick. Wouldn't give him that satisfaction. He'd humiliated me enough.

I stumbled home. Couldn't even bear to think about what had happened. What a fool I'd been. Falling for all his crap. Me. Streetwise Leo who thought he knew everything. Who thought he was being so cool. Armour's boy. Armour's mug, more like.

I can't even remember going home. It was all a blur. I seemed to walk for hours. Found my way back somehow and no one was even waiting up for me. Was my dad home? I didn't know. I came into the house and it all lay quiet. No television. No lights on. I went up to my room and threw myself on the bed. I never wanted to die as much as I did that night. If I hadn't woken up next morning it would have been a blessing. But I did wake up. Still in my clothes, my mouth tasting like the bottom of a budgie's cage.

The sun streamed in the window and birds were singing in the trees outside. Mornings like this were supposed to make you feel better but I felt every bit as bad as I had last night.

Worse. Because daylight seemed to reinforce the fact it was all real. Not a nightmare. It had really happened. And it would never end.

I had to force myself to go downstairs. No one called for me. No Mum yelling upstairs: 'Leo, for the last time, come down and have your breakfast!' Not even David barging into my room wanting me to play one last game with him before he went off for his Saturday swimming lesson with Dad.

They were all at the table when I went into the kitchen. My dad looked as if he had had even less sleep than me.

I didn't know what to say. A thousand sorrys wouldn't be enough. And what would be the point? Because I knew now I would never be free of Armour.

It was my dad who spoke first.

'I went to see my boss last night. And I want you to

know that I got that job fair and square. The man who got the job at the final interview got another job and moved on, and I was next in line. Long before Armour became your pal. So it had nothing to do with him. I owe him nothing. Maybe that first job was thanks to him. But if I was still in that job I would chuck it right now if I thought it had anything to do with Armour. I'm obligated to no man.'

My throat was thick with tears. 'I know, Dad.'

Wee David's face crumpled. 'What's wrong, Dad? Are you mad at Leo?'

My dad leaned over and rumpled David's hair. He didn't answer him. He only said, 'Come on, I'll take you swimming, son.'

David jumped from his chair. 'Is Leo coming?'

My dad shook his head. 'No, Leo's a big boy. Doesn't need his dad any more.'

I'd hurt him so much and I could say nothing to him. My nails bit into my clenched fists. But I didn't know just where to start. Dad just looked at me, picked up David and left.

When they'd gone my mum came and put a hand on my shoulder. 'He's hurt and he doesn't mean that. Your dad'll come round. When does your dad ever stay mad at you?'

Her voice broke and I knew she was ready to cry. She was trying to make me feel better and I didn't deserve that. Because I had hurt her too. She couldn't understand what I had done either. I had hurt the people I loved the most and now there was a chance I could cause them to be hurt even more.

My dad had been so right. Armour had got his hold on me and now he would never let me go.

I left the house and went walking. I needed to think. Think about everything. The trap I had walked right into. I ended up at the river and sat on one of the bollards. Watched the tugs go down the Clyde. Wished I was on one of them.

How could I have been so stupid? Believing Armour was relying on me? Trusting me – falling for his silken words. When he'd only been making me a part in his villainy. How could I ever have convinced myself there was any good in that man? Telling me he was willing to use his own money to pay Nelis so he would move out of town. Make the town a safer place.

If Sean had still been my friend he would have told me. Sean wouldn't have been fooled.

But I had dumped Sean and would I have believed him, anyway?

How could I have convinced myself that Armour would ever do the decent thing when I had seen him blast McCrae to hell, in cold blood?

I had been the witness. I should have run home and told my dad – told the police – no matter the consequences. Instead I had accepted his 'thanks'. His 'favours'. And been drawn into his web as surely as if he was the spider and I was the fly.

Now there was no going back. I was an accessory and couldn't do a thing. He had no intention of helping Mr Sheridan either. All that had been a lie and the poor man would probably be convicted of McCrae's murder and that would be all my fault too.

I could do nothing. Say nothing.

Not even an anonymous phone call to the police.

Look what had happened to the man who'd phoned my dad. Armour had found out who he was and had left him unrecognisable. Hardly looking human at all.

David's wee face flashed before me. David's cute wee face. I felt like screaming. I had to protect him. I could never let Armour hurt him.

And now when Armour let the police know where Nelis's arsenal of guns was, Nelis would be arrested. Armour would take over the whole town. There would be only Armour. Thanks to me.

He was going to grass on Nelis. Ha! That thought made me choke. It was OK for him to grass . . . but not for anyone else.

And all the time I had known where Nelis's guns were hidden. Thank goodness I had never told Armour. At least *that* was something I had done right.

But what was the point? Tonight Armour would know and the police would swoop on the old building and Nelis would be arrested and Armour would take over and . . . It would be all my fault.

Everything spun round in my head, making me dizzy.

How could I have forgotten that he'd shot a man in cold blood? I closed my eyes, and like the rerun of an old movie I was, once again, standing under the trees. Hidden by the darkness, hearing the click of a gun. I saw Armour with the light from the hallway on his face. Saw those rubies of blood spatter over the gun across his face. Saw him wipe the blood from his mouth in disgust, spit on his fingers. Then wrap his hands around the barrel again.

Saw it all in my mind. And a bold plan began to form – a dangerous plan. Could I do it? Dare I?

Yet I knew in that same second nothing was going to stop me.

41

I waited till night crept through the town. I watched it from my bedroom window as it loomed over the river, turning the pink sky to battleship grey and then to ink black. The river was as smooth as smoked glass. The streets fell silent. It was after midnight. And I was ready.

I pulled on my black sweater over my school trousers, the darkest trousers I had. I wanted to move unseen through the streets. I had a long night ahead.

First I had to make sure I wouldn't be missed. I took two pillows from the cupboard and arranged them long ways on the bed. Then I dragged the duvet up and over them. My mum was always complaining that I shouldn't hide myself under the covers.

'You'll suffocate one of these nights,' she always said, cheerily. 'I'll come in here one morning to wake you up and you'll be under there, blue in the face, tongue hanging out of your mouth.'

If she looked into my room in the middle of the night she'd see what she always did – her son tucked tight under the covers. I stood back and surveyed my handiwork. Yes – it could pass for someone lying under there. I was sure of it.

Now all I had to do was get out of the house without anyone hearing me.

They were all asleep as I tiptoed downstairs. I could hear Dad snoring.

I wished I could shut my mind off. Block everything else out. Concentrate on what I had to do. Concentrate only on tonight. I kept my trainers in my hand, remembered to miss the second step from the bottom, the one that squeaked. I made my way into the utility room. Under the sink was something else I had to remember. I pulled out Mum's bag of hospital gloves. Stolen or not, I needed them tonight. I'd seen too many *C.S.I.*s to know I couldn't risk leaving any of my fingerprints anywhere. I shoved a few pairs in my pocket and left the house.

I crept through the streets, taking the path that led through the park. It was popular during the day for mums with their prams and their toddlers. But notorious at night for drug dealing. I would have to be careful.

Was I really doing this? I kept thinking I would wake up any minute back in my own bed. I even nipped at my arm, just in case. But no, this was real.

Halfway through the park I saw a couple of hoodies, bent over, looking on the ground. I darted back into the trees and waited, hoping they would move on soon. I didn't have to wait long. They had only dropped something – their syringes probably – and after a few moments they were gone, stumbling along the path, passing only metres away from me and into the darkness.

After another moment I moved too. I had a way to go. No time to waste. Through the back streets and the alleys. I even planned to take a shortcut through the cemetery.

But I wouldn't stop till I got to where I was going.

I was heading to the spot where I had watched Armour shoot McCrae. I was going back there to retrieve the gun.

Armour had seen me witness the shooting but he hadn't known – couldn't know – that I hadn't run off right away. That I'd stopped for those moments and seen where he'd hidden the murder weapon, wrapped in a black bin bag.

I was in Armour's power, yes. But he was in mine too. I knew where that gun was. And that was the one thing I was sure that even he wasn't aware of.

Had he been back to get it? I'd thought about that all day. Would all this be a wasted journey? I didn't think so. There was still a police presence round the house. He couldn't risk coming back here. Armour anywhere near this area would look suspicious. Then, another thought – would he have got some of his men to get the gun back?

No. He could have had any of his men eliminate McCrae for him. But he had done it himself. He didn't want anyone to know what he'd done. I was the only one who knew.

My gut instinct told me that the gun would still be there. I saw again in my mind the way Armour had wiped the blood from his mouth. The disgust on his face as he had tasted McCrae's blood. He'd spat on his fingers then those same fingers had closed round the butt of that gun. Armour's DNA would be all over it.

That thought kept me going. His DNA would be all over it.

The town was deathly quiet as I crept through the

218

night. I saw no one. Only heard the odd police siren in the distance. Once the screech of wheels of some boy racer as he headed home.

The cemetery was the eeriest part of my journey. If I could have avoided it I would have. But it was a great shortcut. I climbed over one of the gates at the side and stood for a moment looking around.

They're all dead in here, I kept telling myself. But I couldn't get out of my head the zombie films Sean and I loved to watch. Remembered how the zombies clawed their way towards the surface, dragged themselves up from their graves. Began their shambling walk towards their human prey, hungry for warm human flesh. My flesh.

I began to run. The sooner I was out of this cemetery, the better I'd feel.

Once I stopped and almost screeched out when I heard the bushes rustle behind me. I swung round expecting to see a horde of zombies heading my way. They'd never catch me, I thought. They were always too slow. Then I remembered that in the latest batch of zombie movies those zombies could run.

Of course there was no one behind me. Some wee animal – a squirrel, a cat – had hidden in the bushes probably. More scared of me than I could ever be of it. Zombies didn't exist. They weren't real. The dead couldn't come alive. I should only be afraid of real villains – like Armour.

But I kept running anyway.

I had another wall to climb to get out. Landed right in the middle of more bushes. They seemed to bounce me on to the ground. Something fell from my pocket. A quick search told me what it was. My torch. I sat for a moment, trying to get my breath back.

My torch was gone. I knelt on the ground, tried to feel around for it. But there were too many bushes, too many cracks in the ground. It could be anywhere. It would take ages to find it. And I didn't have ages.

Finally I gave up. I wouldn't need it, I told myself as I moved on. I knew where I was going and what I had to do. I would not need the torch.

Once out of the cemetery I ran through the back gardens. At last I could see the wall behind the Chinese takeaway where I had hidden that night. This was it.

I checked all around. Could see no one. I took a deep breath and crept closer.

Half of me, the half with that wild imagination, expected to find Armour still crouched there, caught in time. The gun enveloped in black still in his hand.

But of course there was no one. Nothing. Only litter and the odd plastic bag caught on the trees. Only a weird kind of quiet – as if the world was waiting to see what would happen next.

42

I crouched down, breathless, and crawled towards the spot. The end of the pipe was barely visible. It was stuffed with crisp packets – you would hardly know a pipe was there at all. I almost missed it myself. But when I spidered my hands and ran them along the surface of the ground my fingers caught on the jagged edges. I pulled the packets free, exposed the black hole. This was the moment I had to brace myself for. The moment I put my hand inside that long black tube. Thank goodness I had the protection of the gloves. Thin enough so that I could feel anything, yet with a slim layer to protect me if there was anything else down there waiting to bite me.

I took a deep breath, flexed my fingers and let them tiptoe inside the pipe. It was drier in there than I had expected. Not filled with grimy water, just damp. But I could feel no rifle butt wrapped in plastic.

Had he moved it? Come here one dark night just like me and taken the gun?

I almost drew my hand out. Coming here was a waste of time.

But Armour's arm was longer than mine. He could reach further. He would have pushed it down as far as it would go.

Another horrifying thought – had he pushed it in so far that I could never reach it?

I was only a boy. What was I doing here? There was nothing I could do. It was too late.

I saw the horrifying future. Armour would grass on Nelis. Nelis would be arrested. And then Armour would go after my dad . . . And David . . .

No! I couldn't ever let that happen. I couldn't stop now.

And all the time these terrifying thoughts were tumbling in my head, my fingers stretched further down that black hole.

Every second I was terrified of what else I might find. Rats could have made their home down there . . . or a whole nest of spiders . . . or – my imagination went haywire. Or some kind of alien creature lurking in the dark, waiting for some idiot's hand to come close so it could grasp at my fingers. Envelop them. Suck its way up my arm. Take over my whole body . . .

NO!

I jerked my fingers back. I couldn't do this.

But Armour had done it.

By now I was lying flat on the ground, my arm in the pipe up to my elbow. I had to go further. My fingers splayed inside searching all around. Didn't want to miss anything down there. I pushed my arm in even further. Tried to block every terror from my mind.

I was in up to my shoulder and still nothing. It was gone for sure, I thought, and then, just when I thought I could reach no further, my fingers touched something cold. Something plastic.

I held my breath. I would have to push my arm in even further to get a grip so I could yank it out. I was so flat on the ground now that my chin was touching the pipe. But now all I had was one thought. I had found it. It was still here.

At last my fingers closed round the barrel. I began to pull. It didn't move. It was wedged in tight. Surely after all this I'd be able to pull it out.

Panic began to set in. To be this close, and fail?

No. I wouldn't let that happen. I pulled again. Then again. And at last it seemed to come alive. Jerked with my hand. Came loose.

Now I had a firmer grip. I inched it back down the pipe. Didn't want the bin bag ripped or torn. Didn't want the evidence contaminated.

And I *had* the evidence of Armour's guilt, clutched round my fingers. I had it almost in my hand.

At last it came, emerging from the pipe like something newborn.

But it was a gun wrapped in black and it was evil.

No. The gun itself wasn't evil – just lying here on the ground it was harmless. It was the hands it could fall into and how they would use it that would turn it into something evil.

I sat up and leaned against the wall. I pulled the gun on to my lap. It was heavier than I'd imagined it would be. And I knew in that moment I never wanted to be near a gun again. Never wanted to touch one, or feel the terror of what it was capable of. My mind played over and over the moment I had seen that gun come to life. It's life had been someone's death. McCrae's.

Well now it could help put the man responsible behind bars.

I had the power in my hand – but how to use it?

I had thought long and hard about what to do next, as I had sat by the river. Gone over all my options.

I had thought at first I would call the police to tell them where to find the gun. But a call could be traced. And so soon after my meeting with Armour, he would surely put two and two together and know, or suspect, it was me who'd grassed on him.

No. Had to keep my family – David – safe.

Should I walk into a police station and calmly hand it over?

There'd be too many questions. And Armour would know I was the one who had brought it in.

David's face in front of me again. Smiling, laughing. No. I had to protect him.

Should I leave the gun somewhere for the police to find?

I had dismissed that right away. Too much chance of some lowlife or some drug addict finding it first. It would once again be in dangerous hands and, worse, the evidence of Armour's guilt might be wiped clean.

Or should I hide the gun somewhere myself? Use it as my insurance that Armour would leave my family alone? Leave David alone?

Don't think I didn't consider that. Blackmailing Armour. Sweet revenge.

But then I'd never be free of him. And even worse, it would make me almost as bad as he was. Bring me down to his level.

No. I had to do the right thing. Or at least, the only thing that was left available to me.

I had to make sure Armour was brought to justice but in a way he would never know it was me.

He was meeting Nelis at 3 a.m. At the Willow Bar. Armour would want to see the merchandise he was pretending he would buy. And as soon as he found out where the guns were, he'd send the police there to find them.

A daring plan had begun to form in my mind this morning by the river. But it was too dangerous. Too scary. And I had racked my brain to come up with something better, some safer way. But I couldn't. If there was an alternative I wasn't clever enough to think of it.

In that moment I wished Sean was there beside me. To talk to, to discuss it with. The two of us could always figure things out. Making up stories for our adventures as we searched the old derelict properties.

It was thinking of Sean that gave me the courage to

move on. I would think of this as one of our games. As if Sean was moving in the dark with me, giving me courage. I wouldn't be so afraid then.

I stood up, held the gun in my arms as if it were a baby, and I began to run.

43

The town was still silent, still dark. I was on a deadline, a race against time. Sean and I always had a race against time. And that memory kept me going too. I ran through the back roads, the back gardens of tenements. Leaping over walls, crawling through hedges. It was in the early hours of a Sunday, and there was still people about in town. I passed teenage girls giggling their way home from the local disco. They didn't see me. Too busy texting on their mobiles to notice anything. The odd taxi flew past and when I heard one coming I'd flatten myself against a wall till it had roared off into the distance again. I had a gun in my arms. I didn't want anyone to remember seeing me. I had to stay focused.

I took my life in my hands, crossing over the railway tracks and under the bridge. I was leaving McCrae's territory now. Nelis and Armour both wanted control of it. How could I have doubted anything else? I had always known these things. Armour wanted to take over from McCrae, so did Nelis. Armour wanting peace? How could I have been so stupid as to believe that?

I could have told you, pal. Sean's voice. I could almost hear it break the night silence. Yes. Sean would have kept me right if I could have told him what I'd witnessed. But I'd been afraid to. Afraid I might put him in danger too.

No point thinking about that now, I reminded myself. Keep moving. Heading for Nelis's territory.

For a moment I stopped to get my breath back. At the top of the hill the views were stupendous. On a clear night like this with the sky so close I felt I could touch the stars. I could see right up the river – could see Dumbarton Rock and the lights on the Erskine Bridge. There were tankers anchored in the Clyde waiting to go into the container terminal. Everything at peace.

Except my heart. Beating in double-quick time. Urging me on.

I checked my watch. It was almost two. So little time to do what I had to do. Armour had a plan but so did I. And if my plan worked Armour's devious little scheme was going to backfire. Blow up in his face.

If it worked. If I wasn't too late.

What if he'd changed the time he was meant to meet Nelis? What if Armour had met him at midnight? What if he'd already called the police? What if they were already swarming all over Clyde Terrace?

But they weren't. In front of me at last, the derelict tenement building. Lying quiet and empty. I lay flat and silent in the jungle of grass and waited. I checked my watch again. Ten minutes to three. I wouldn't, shouldn't have long to wait. They were to meet at the old Willow Bar, but I had worked out that it would take them at least ten minutes to get here.

In fact, it only took them five. It was Armour I saw first. He strode along the terrace as if it was the middle of the day. As if he had nothing to fear. Nelis walked ahead of him, more wary. Looking back, talking to Armour. I could hear nothing of what they were saying. But I didn't need to hear. I knew what they were talking about. Guns. Nelis's guns.

They stopped at the entrance to the first house. Both of them looked round, checking no one was about. I pressed myself further down into the overgrown grass. They had none of their henchmen with them. This was something they wanted to do alone. Nelis knew how to get in. He didn't need any loose panel. He stood in front of the door and it opened like magic. He stepped inside and with one more glance around to make sure he wasn't being watched, Armour followed him.

They seemed to be in there for ever. The sweat poured from me. I couldn't bear this waiting. 'I could never have made a real commando,' I silently whispered to Sean. 'Not got the nerve for it.'

Finally they did come out. Nelis first. I knew right away he had been paid. There was a smug look on his face. And he was stuffing an envelope into his pocket. Armour wouldn't have given him all of the money – not until the guns were safely in his keep. But Nelis had been given a deposit at least. Armour came out next. He looked as if he was laughing. As if something had struck him as funny. Nelis turned and laughed too – as if he knew what the joke was. Then Nelis held out his hand and Armour held out his. Two villains shaking on a deal. Only Nelis didn't know what the real deal was.

They only stood together for a few more seconds. Then they moved off, in different directions. Nelis perhaps to spend some of his money. And Armour to make a very important phone call.

I couldn't wait for long. Didn't know how much time I had. I had to get inside there as soon as possible before the police descended on the place.

Could I do it again? Unseen? Had to try.

I said a prayer. There had to be a saint up there who could help me. There was a patron saint for everything. There must be a patron saint for sneaking into derelict properties.

Just in case there wasn't, I decided to cut out the middle man. Go to the Big Man himself.

'God, help me to do the right thing.' It was all I said. Couldn't think of anything else.

Then I took a deep breath and headed for the house.

My plan was simple enough. I would slip Armour's gun with his prints, his saliva, McCrae's blood – every bit of evidence against him – slip it down under the floorboards with Nelis's guns. When the police came after Armour's call they would find them all. They would have Nelis, thanks to Armour. And they would have Armour himself and all the evidence to prove he was McCrae's killer. It would look as if, unknown to Armour, Nelis had had the murder weapon all the time.

That they had perhaps worked together to get rid of McCrae and then had turned on each other.

And no one would ever know I had anything to do with it.

44

Good plan, eh?

But first I had to get in, hide the gun, pray no one caught me.

I crossed the back greens and flattened myself against the wall of the building. I'd been going over in my mind just how I had got in there the first time. Through the loose steel panel boarding up one of the windows on the ground floor.

It was easy to find. The only one with any kind of gap. So slim that only a boy like me could get through. Nelis, of course, had his own way in – a way he could secure and know his stash was safe.

I reached up for the window sill and pulled my way up. Not easy with a gun in one hand. I squeezed my way inside. And dropped to the floor. I was in the old kitchen again. I waited. Waited for a horde of

Nelis's men to jump me.

But Armour wouldn't have come in if any of Nelis's men were there. Or he wouldn't have come out again. I waited. The house was silent. Nothing. Nelis had left it unguarded again.

Or had he?

I cursed myself for losing my torch. This was when I needed it. I hesitated – to give my eyes time to become accustomed to the darkness. There was a door ahead of me lying half open, and beyond that the room with the loose floorboards. And under those floorboards . . .

Why wasn't anyone guarding this place? It was hard to believe Nelis had left it unguarded for all these weeks.

I took a few tiptoed steps forward. Imagined again a whole gang of Nelis's men waiting for me, guns aimed straight at me.

But when I pulled the door open wider there was still no sound. The room was empty. Pitch-black and empty.

I imagined Nelis and Armour when they were in here not so long ago – Armour demanding to see the merchandise. Nelis hauling the boards across to show him what he had.

Why wasn't anyone guarding this place? The thought wouldn't go away.

Maybe he didn't need *people* to guard here. He couldn't trust people. Who else would he leave on guard ?

I was almost stopped in my tracks.

Dogs.

Rottweilers. Dobermanns.

I held my breath, listening for a sound. A low growl. The sound of jaws dripping. I looked around, looking for two pinpoints of light watching me. But there was nothing.

They would have been alerted as soon as I'd jumped into the kitchen, surely?

There couldn't be any dogs here.

Nelis was just stupid. I'd always thought so. He thought because everyone knew this was his place he didn't need guards.

My foot brushed against something as I walked on. I didn't look to see what it might be. My eyes homed in on that loose floorboard. I saw nothing else. It had been lifted and now lay on top of the floor.

The guns were still there. And there was something menacing about them even as they lay still and unused.

I crouched down. I slipped a second pair of surgical gloves on, just to be on the safe side. Didn't want my fingerprints left anywhere here.

I dropped to my knees to crawl closer when my foot brushed again against something metal. This time I reached back to move whatever it was aside. Not afraid. Not thinking.

Should have looked first.

There was the sudden snap of metal, missing my fingers by a centimetre. I flinched back. Another terrifying snap next to me. I froze. Saw what it was at last.

A trap. A metal trap, its jaws now closed tight.

I looked all around the room. It seemed to become clear as day all at once. As if moonlight had lit it with a strange silver glow.

Nelis hadn't left anything human to guard his stash.

He had just booby-trapped the whole room.

45

My whole body froze. I'd read about your hair standing on end, but this was the first time I knew what that meant. I knew – should have known – it wouldn't be this easy.

I had walked into this room, managing by sheer luck so far to miss the traps that were set here. Steel teeth everywhere, ready to snap shut. Animal traps. Man traps. We were close to farmland here, easy for Nelis to get his hands on them. Easy and deadly. They hadn't been here when I had found the guns. Nelis probably hadn't had time to set them then.

Now I knew what it was that had struck Armour as funny. I saw them again, him and Nelis, laughing as they came out of the building. I could almost hear Armour congratulating him on laying the traps to deter any intruders, telling him how clever he was, and Nelis too stupid to realise the joke was about to be on him.

Although at this minute it was no joke for me either. If my leg had been caught in that trap, it would have been the end for me and my plan. My blood, my DNA – probably my dead body – would have been found here in this room when the police swooped.

I was afraid to move. Wasn't hard. My body was like a block of ice.

What was I going to do? If only I'd had the torch I could at least see what I was doing. See exactly where those traps where. And how to avoid them. I couldn't trust to luck again.

But I had no torch. There was no way I was going to get out of here avoiding those traps. I was done for.

Deal with it, Leo. It was Sean in my mind, telling me I had to find a way.

OK, smart alec, I barked back at him. *Any more advice?*

Get that gun in with the others. That's your mission. I was so sure I heard Sean's voice I looked around.

Yes, he was right. I'd come here to put that gun under the floorboards with the others and no amount of booby traps was going to stop me.

That gun was going to convict Armour. And if by any chance I was still here. I'd just have to find a way to explain it.

I wasn't going to be here!

I would find a way out, some way.

I turned and moved warily forward, one sliding movement after the other. From here I was almost sure if I leaned forward, reached out, I could move that floorboard further out of the way.

Snap!

The jaws of another trap snapped shut as soon as my foot touched it.

It was impossible to stay still then. I was too scared. I jerked to the side and behind me. Close to my hands, too close, another bite of a trap. They were everywhere. I felt as if I was in shark-infested waters.

I was burning up and freezing at the same time. But I knew I couldn't stop now. I had a mission. I focused on the open floor. Tried to wipe everything else out of my mind. I wanted to throw the gun in there and run but it had to be secure with the rest of the arsenal. The black bag intact, the evidence uncontaminated. I held the gun tightly, leaned closer and edged the floorboard aside.

It seemed to fly in the air as one of the traps closed on it. It took every bit of nerve I had not to flinch then. If it fell and hit me I'd lose my balance for sure. Those waiting steel jaws wouldn't miss me then. The floorboard fell with a crack and a snap, caught by another trap.

For an age, I couldn't move. Didn't want to move. Too terrified.

Almost there. Sean's voice urging me on.

He was right. I was almost there. I leaned forward as far as I could and pushed the gun in with the others. It slipped inside easily as if it was being sucked in, as if it belonged there.

It was done. The best way I could.

'Mission accomplished,' I said softly. Well, almost.

All I had to do now, was get out of this room in one piece.

Well I had managed to get this far, hadn't I?

What would Sean and I have done in such a situation? And it came to me at once what to do.

When soldiers were in a minefield they would lie flat on their bellies and crawl forward, pushing their backpacks ahead of them, using them to clear a safe route. The trap closest to me – the one near my hands, was already snapped shut. If I pushed that in front of me it would surely clear a path for me as I inched my way towards the kitchen. Through the open door I could make out a slit of pale moonlight. I kept my eye on that. Hope. Escape. That's where I was heading.

I lay even flatter. Touched the cold steel of the trap. Took a deep breath. Inch by inch I slithered forward. The trap that could have killed me moments ago became my saviour. It touched another trap and it too snapped closed. It pushed others aside safely out of my way.

It must have only taken minutes but it seemed like hours before I reached the door at last. The trap edged it open wider. Still I lay flat, afraid to move a fraction out of the path laid for me. Not until I was safely into the kitchen did I jump to my feet. I began to shake. Shook so hard I thought I wouldn't stop. An earthquake moved inside me. I'd never get into anything like this again.

I wanted to be a boy again, and do the daft, crazy things that Sean and I loved doing.

I could hardly pull open the steel panel my hands shook so much. I'd never make it home. I was sure of it. I stumbled as I fell to the ground from the window. But I had to make it home. I was bathed in ice-cold sweat but I couldn't rest yet. I had to get away from here. I began to run.

Home.

I couldn't wait to get home.

46

My mum had to wake me next morning. Calling to me from the doorway of my bedroom. Lucky for me she didn't come closer. I had slept in my clothes. Crept back into the house sometime in the middle of the night, terrified my dad would be waiting up for me. That thought scared me more than anything else that night. For how would I explain where I'd been?

But the house had been silent. No one was waiting for me. No one had missed me. I was still in the bad books.

It was only when I was back in my own bedroom that the full force of what I'd done hit me. I began to shake once again and couldn't stop. I shivered, so cold my teeth began to chatter. Nerves I suppose, catching up with me. I climbed into bed and pulled the duvet up around me. Just wanted to get warm, planned to change into my pyjamas as soon as there was some heat in me. And that's the last thing I remember.

My dad was working this Sunday but he hadn't left for work when I went downstairs for breakfast. I knew he was waiting for me.

'You look like death.' First thing he said.

Mum came right over to me, felt my brow. 'You feeling OK?'

'Probably heard of the arrest,' my dad snapped at me. He nodded over to the radio. 'Just been on the news.'

I caught my breath – it had happened already! The police must have arrived just after I'd left last night.

I stumbled into a chair and Dad took my shock for sympathy. 'Och, don't worry. It's not your pal, Armour. It's Nelis . . . and I'm sure he'll find a way to get out of it.'

'They found guns – a whole blinking houseful of them,' my mum said. 'I don't think he'll get out of this one.'

My dad went back to his paper. 'I hope not.'

I found my voice at last, but it came out as if it had been scraped with sandpaper. 'Armour's not my pal, Dad.' I had to make him understand I knew exactly what Armour was. 'I know Armour's not a good man. I'm sorry, Dad.'

Dad stared at me. My sudden apology took him by surprise.

'You were right, Dad. He never does anything without wanting something in return. He's a nasty bit of work. I –' I was stumbling over the words. 'I don't know how I ever thought he could be anything different. I was stupid, Dad.'

David sat, still in his pyjamas, looking from me to Dad. Waiting for what was going to happen next. It seemed to me my dad was taking a long time to say anything.

It was my mum who broke the silence. 'For goodness' sake, Dave, the boy's trying to apologise. Don't sit there like a big drink of water. Say something.'

My dad looked at her and I could tell he was trying to keep his face straight. Never could manage it with my mum. For her the ghost of a smile appeared. But when he glanced back at me his face was grim again. Too soon for him to forgive me.

'I know you're a good boy, Leo. I never doubted that.'

'I'll never see him again. I promise, Dad. I promise.'

My throat hurt because I wanted to cry so much. I think my dad did too.

He nodded. His eyes filled up. 'I'll see you when I

come back in from work. We'll talk about it then. OK?'

Better than OK, I thought because my dad was going to give me another chance.

David jumped from his chair. 'Dad, Dad! I'm a good boy too.'

Dad lifted him high. 'You're a superhero, David. They're always good boys.'

David turned and looked at me. 'Leo's a superhero as well, Dad.'

Dad looked at me, said nothing. It was too soon for me to move to superhero status again.

It was all over the town, the arrest. Nelis and umpteen of his men in police custody. Someone had grassed on him. Told the police about his guns. I saw Sean at Mass and he watched me, as if I was part of it.

It was the longest day of my life. Why hadn't they arrested Armour? I waited for news of Armour being taken in for questioning. What if they hadn't found the gun? What if some rookie cop had pulled it from the black bin bag, thinking it was just another gun in the stash? What if . . . what if . . . what if . . . ?

The 'what if's drove me crazy all day.

But I needn't have worried. By evening Armour had

been arrested too. The town was buzzing with the news. No one seemed to doubt the story. It was Armour who had grassed on Nelis. The police had monitored the call, had prints of Armour's voice. He had told the police about Nelis's arsenal of guns little knowing that, according to a police statement, Nelis had already found the gun that Armour had used on McCrae. Hidden it among his own. Armour's fingerprints, his DNA, had all been found on the gun.

Now, according to the rumours, they were screaming vengeance at each other.

I watched Armour's arrest on television. He stepped through his front door, hands cuffed behind his back, and was led from the house with the stone lions at the gates. He looked angry.

A crowd had gathered outside, and I wished I'd been there standing in that silent crowd, watching him, and when he passed, do you know what I would have done? I would have winked – and he would have known that I was responsible. Me. Leo McCabe. He would have known that it was because of me he was being arrested. Because of me he'd been tricked and would spend the next few years in prison.

And even thinking it I knew I could never have gone

there, never let him know. To keep myself safe – my family safe, David safe. I could never let anyone know.

Armour could never know it was me.

And I wanted so much for him to know. One wink would have shown him who'd won in the end.

But I could never do it. I could never tell.

That was the only way to stay safe.

I'd never be able to tell my dad everything, that would always have to be my secret. But now I had the time – the chance – to prove to him that I was a son he could be proud of again. I was determined to do that, no matter how long it took.

Nelis and Armour were gone. The town was free of them at last. And my dad was determined that no one else would take their place. My dad and lots of other dads and mums in our town.

There will always be villains, I know that. But there will always be heroes too, like my dad. A real man.

In the next few days Mr Sheridan was released. It turned out that Armour had manufactured evidence of his involvement in the shooting. He had even supplied the false witnesses who said they'd seen him in the area.

How could I ever have believed that Armour would make sure he was freed? How could I have been so stupid?

My only excuse is . . . I wanted to protect my family.

But I had been responsible for ridding the town of him. I had turned the tables on him. But I couldn't tell anyone.

Or could I?

There was maybe one person I could tell. The only person I could trust with that knowledge. I could tell him now and he wouldn't be in any danger and he'd maybe understand why I'd done it. Why I'd done so many things. And why I couldn't tell him before.

Just one person. Sean.

And maybe, just maybe – if I was really lucky – he'd be my mate again.

Not right away, I knew that. It might take time. But I could wait. I would work hard to prove he could trust me again.

It took all my nerve – more than I needed to go out that night I planted the gun – to go to Sean's house.

I bought myself a packet of Mint Imperials to give me courage and headed for his street. I rang the bell and after an age it was Sean himself who opened the door. As if he'd seen me coming up the path, and had considered ignoring me.

I tried not to stumble over the words. I was so afraid he'd tell me to bog off before I got the chance to say anything.

'There's something I have to tell you, Sean.'

He looked at me. Said nothing for a long time. I was sure he was about to shut the door in my face, but he only shrugged his shoulders.

'Suppose you better come in, then,' he said.

And I stepped inside.